A POSH MURDER

REX AND THE DOWAGER BOOK 1

KEITH FINNEY

Flegg
Publishing

AN INVITATION

This is your personal invitation to join my exclusive
Readers' Club.
Receive free, exclusive content only available to members,
including short stories and more.
To join, click on the link towards the end of the book and
you're in!

1

QUITE A PICNIC

'Are you certain the gentleman is dead, Rex? Perhaps he merely sleeps, albeit in a peculiar position.'

There was no escaping the fact. Before us lay the prone body of a man I took to be a little older than my twenty-one years. His unnatural position, face down over the immense girth of a fallen tree by a beautiful lake, legs akimbo and left arm outstretched, gave the gentleman – for that's what he appeared to be from the quality of his attire – the look of someone who had attempted to simulate the breaststroke with disastrous consequences.

I noted two curious facts: the surprised expression on his motionless face, and the second, that his left hand rested palm-upward with his index and middle finger elegantly extended in the manner of a thespian acting out his tragic demise.

I recounted these facts to my employer, Eleanor, Dowager Duchess of Drakeford, an amateur sleuth of great repute in certain circles.

'Many people who meet their end suddenly, bear the countenance of yonder fellow. It is because the individual thinks to themselves, "So this is what it feels like", or exhibits utter surprise that an acquaintance is about to do them in, so to speak.'

Before I had time to gather my thoughts, HG asked that I nip back to the Rolls to recover a heavy wool blanket. At first, I thought it might be to cover the deceased gentlemen out of respect. Not so. My Lady bade me lay the hand-knitted Shetland weave on a bare patch of soil by the water's edge, whereupon she'd inadvertently disturbed a colony of red ants. The blanket proved a perfect antidote to their shenanigans as HG tucked into her favourite sandwiches: smoked salmon with a hint of Fortnum and Mason special relish and sea-salt sent from the Outer Hebrides on annual consignment.

'Do you think the gentleman has been here long?' I asked.

Without breaking stride from sipping her specially mixed Twinings English Afternoon Tea blend, HG estimated his final decline as being one hour, fifty-seven minutes earlier. When I enquired about the precise nature of her calculation, HG remarked the man's frozen facial features and rigid hand bore all the hallmarks of rigour mortice having recently set in.

Rigour mortice was a revelation to me. Although having reached my majority the previous month, the only dead body I'd hitherto observed was that of my Uncle Cedric, who had died of a troublesome liver and was secured into his coffin in what I thought indecent haste.

His wake at the Dog and Duck was a splendid event, though it was later said the owner fell into a rapid decline, as did his profits, once Uncle Cedric ceased favouring the establishment with his business.

Having replenished HG's tea and arranged the dainty

cakes on a silver platter to her liking, I inspected the unfortunate gentleman. I gazed in wonder that not a hair on his head was out of place, save for a gaping wound along his neat centre parting. Yet I saw not the faintest of marks upon his hands.

'It seems to me, HG, that he failed to put up any resistance to the violent onslaught. Odd, don't you think, when someone is intent on bumping you off?'

The dowager took some persuading to put down her iced fancy and entertain my deduction. However, dispatched to the Rolls-Royce for a replacement fancy, I returned to observe the dowager getting to her feet quiet energetically for a woman of advancing years with a clicky hip.

I now witnessed the master at work. Disturbed from her recreational pursuits, HG circled the body like a ravenous lion stalking its prey.

She gesticulated as if bashing someone over the head by raising her hand and allowing it to descend violently. Alas, this caused HG's iced fancy to fly from her iron grip and hit the unfortunate fellow square on the left temple. 'I had been enjoying that,' she remarked.

Reaching into the inside pocket of the fellow's jacket, HG withdrew an expensive-looking leather wallet and opened it. 'His name is Ambrose Bagley,' she said, inspecting his motor vehicle driving licence. 'Born April 1899, so he was twenty-three. He lived at a good address in Knightsbridge, I notice.'

As she methodically sifted through each compartment, two five-pound notes came to light, as well as four one-penny red postage stamps and a folded newspaper cutting.

'How curious.' The dowager handed me the sliver of paper. One side contained an advertisement for 'Blenkin's

Elixir, sure to keep you moving', which I presumed was not pertinent to the matter at and. On the other, among a short list of announcements, one stood out with two short, heavy lines having been drawn in the margin. The advert read:

Will you at ten? W. Halt

In the final compartment, HG recovered a ticket stub. It pointed to a train journey from London Charing Cross terminating locally. In tiny writing in one corner, someone, presumably the deceased, had scribbled 'Arrive 10.42 am'.

'I estimate the walk from the station to this location took him not more than fifteen minutes. Given it's now one thirty by the church clock and we found the fellow not ten minutes since, he cannot have croaked it before 11.07 am. It is clear to me he won't recover. In fact, I doubt he knew what hit him, although I'm sure he knew precisely who finished him. Your excellent and most astute observation tells me this chap made no attempt to fend off his attacker.'

I marvelled at the skill and diligence that HG devoted to the stranger. After all, we could have simply packed our things away and returned to Drakeford, seat of the dowager's deceased husband's family since 1216. Not to put too fine a point on matters, the stranger was as dead as it was possible to be, so no further harm could befall him.

However, that was not how HG saw things. As she was often to remind me over the years, her motto remained invenire omnes: 'to find out all', or FOA as she preferred to say.

Surveying the sombre scene, HG instructed we should repair to our host for the weekend, Colonel Crispen Percival-Travers (Retired) at Bircham Manor, in whose extensive grounds we happened upon the tragic Ambrose.

'Do hurry, Rex, or we shall be late. Crispen does a wonderful lunch. Absolutely famed throughout the Home Counties.'

My instructions clear, I secured the wicker picnic basket on the running board of the Rolls, ensured the dowager remained comfortably seated in the limousine's rear and rejoined the mile-and-a-half of newly laid tarmacadam drive that led to the front entrance of the manor.

'Make haste, Rex; we must advise the colonel of our discovery and insist he calls for Whipple of Scotland Yard at once.'

———

SEVERAL WELL-TURNED-OUT LADIES AND GENTLEMEN MILLED around the front entrance as house staff removed luggage from a variety of fine vehicles. Of these, one or two appeared to disturb HG's otherwise calm countenance.

'I see he's invited the Watkins-Simms twins. Mark my words; sparks, not to say fisticuffs, shall fly before the weekend is over.'

HG pointed to the younger twin and his wife, who I thought an unusual match. The husband was a small chap with a balding crown, his dignity preserved by a severe comb-over topping a sombre day suit and Oxford shoes. The man twitched from time to time when his wife offered an icy stare.

Although they appeared to be a similar age, which I estimated to be the wrong side of fifty, the lady wore an ensemble reminiscent of the young ladies known as 'flappers', a point not lost on two such girls pointing and giggling from the safety of a dashing Bentley, which looked resplendent in its livery of British Racing Green.

The elder of the Watkins-Simms, on the other hand, appeared sporty and full of the joys of spring in their matching tennis whites and swinging their rackets with such gusto that the wife almost clipped a footman removing crocodile skin weekend cases from their Citroen motor vehicle.

'Those two hate each other. Twin brothers, would you believe. I've tried several times to effect a reconciliation but the soberly dressed one, and eleven minutes the younger, refuses all efforts. Still, what can you do when, for the sake of the time it takes to prepare and cook a couple of good omelettes, the elder inherits their father's considerable estate.'

I thought the cooking analogy a funny one for HG to choose, since she once confided in me that the nearest she'd come to cooking was heating a kettle on the great range of Drakeford Hall. All appeared well, she recounted, until a hissing sound became apparent and on inspection, so insufficient was the water in the brass kettle to sustain being heated that a hole appeared in its substantial base.

'We must find the colonel. There isn't a second to lose,' announced HG as she neglected to wait for me to open the car door for her, instead launching herself forth so that two nearby footmen almost bumped heads when bowing, so flustered were they at the dowager's rapid progress through the open front doors to the manor house.

Wasting no time in following my employer, Lomas, the butler, did all in his power to bar my entry to the grand house. 'To the kitchen door, my man,' he said in a lofty tone.

Fortunately, HG remained within hearing range of the remark and educated the aged, and I thought slightly tipsy, butler. 'Rex is my man. In fact, he is my Man of all Works, and must attend me.'

Lomas clearly took the dowager's remark with disdain as he elevated his head and gave the air an exaggerated sniff.

'Am I understood?' insisted HG.

'As you wish, Your Grace,' came the surly reply as he shifted half a pace to his right and eyed me from head to foot as I passed into the Jacobean entrance hall, resplendent with a grand ebonised oak staircase and panelling, soot-scarred from a large open fire.

'What kind of a job title is that, Eleanor?' The booming voice of the colonel filled the vast space as a rotund elderly gentleman in a pair of plus fours and Norfolk shooting jacket bounded down the wide stairs with such gusto that his complexion bore a distinctly purple hue by the time he kissed My Lady on both cheeks and pointed a gnarled fore-finger at me.

Two worldly-wise Irish wolfhounds bolted for the great hall as the colonel stepped across the stone-paved reception area to give me a closer inspection. HG said later this was because they thought the colonel's appearance meant exercise, something she gathered they preferred not to partake in.

'Man of All Works, you say?' The colonel strode purposefully over to me and did a turn about my person as if inspecting a new beast for his famous herd of Aberdeen Angus cattle. 'Does he cook? I've heard that some of the smaller households of the middling sort employ a *Maid* of all Works. That is, a single female servant to run the house. Never a man.'

HG set about her host. 'Well, since my eldest son inherited the estate, I live in modest accommodation.'

The colonel continued to press his logic. 'Eleanor, I understand you have two gardeners, a cook and kitchen assistant, plus many other house staff. Hardly a small entourage, I think?'

The dowager dismissed his claim with a flick of her gloved hand and bade the butler furnish her with a telephone. 'Rex tends to my needs when away from the house, so you shall see him in various states of attire so as not to disturb the senseless sensibilities of your other guests.' She gave the colonel no opportunity to seek further clarification before continuing her forceful narration. 'Listen to me, Crispin; Rex and I have found a deceased person on your land and you must allow me to ring Scotland Yard forthwith. Where is that telephone?'

The colonel's face was a picture as he hurried the butler, whose scowl seemed permanent, to comply with the dowager's request, while trying to make sense of the disturbing information.

'A deceased person, you say. Do we know him?'

HG shook her head. 'It is one Ambrose Bagley of Knightsbridge. I once knew a Bagshot who disgraced himself in front of Her Majesty, Queen Victoria, but Bagley? I think not.'

Colonel Percival-Travis appeared nonplussed. 'No, can't say I know the family either. I wonder what he was doing on my land. Too much trespassing nowadays if you ask me.'

Just then his wife, Augustine, breezed into the hall carrying an elegant vase full of deep red roses, smelling their scent as she glided across the stone floor. 'Don't be so silly, darling. Of course we know the Bagleys. They stayed with us during Wimbledon. Don't you remember, the boy has an excellent backhand.'

'Not now he hasn't,' replied the colonel, which I thought in poor taste.

'Why ever not, Crispin; is he injured?'

I attempted to catch the dowager's attention, except she was too busy supervising the now cowering butler in placing the telephone at a comfortable height to save HG's clicky hip from playing up.

'Do you never listen, my darling? The boy isn't injured; he's bally-well dead. Eleanor is, as we speak, in conference with Whipple of the Yard.' The colonel pointed to the dowager as she dismissed the butler with a flea in his ear.

'Where did you get him from, for heaven's sake, Augustine?'

The colonel's wife sighed at HG and waved her free hand as if wishing the problem might go away. 'I know, Eleanor, but good staff are difficult to find nowadays. However, on the plus side, he's jolly good at banging the dinner gong on time, so at least we eat hot food these days. Anyway, I have much to do if we are to be ready for all our guests. Please give my regards to Mr Whipple-Yard, though I have to say I consider it a strange name.'

———

BY THE TIME I COLLECTED INSPECTOR WHIPPLE AND HIS TWO constables from the station, deposited them at the manor, changed into my day suit and entered the orangery, afternoon tea had already begun.

'Haven't I met you before? You look familiar. Have I nicked you for anything?' asked Whipple with a certain sharpness to his voice as I progressed through the glass and cast-iron marvel, collected a plate and transited several sandwich and cake stands to fulfil HG's catering needs.

I gave a polite bow from the neck and explained I had recently delivered him from the train station.

'And now you eat cucumber sandwiches and Victoria sponge with your betters. How extraordinary.'

Used to such a reaction in the short time I'd enjoyed the dowager's patronage, I continued about my business.

'Her Grace calls him her Man of All Works,' explained the colonel before asking Whipple if he wished to divest himself of his heavy overcoat and trilby, if only to avert heat-stroke in the humid atmosphere of the glazed construction.

He refused the colonel's suggestion and, instead, continued to sweat profusely, leaving a trail of sweat droplets from his glistening nose on the red-tiled floor as he moved around.

Several minutes later, the Whipple called the assembly to order. As he did so, one of the Irish wolfhounds dragged a silver server containing Coleman's mustard under the table behind the police officer.

'My name is Whipple; Whipple of the Yard.'

As I monitored the wolfhound, I glimpsed the colonel's wife straining to speak.

'Of which yard? Do we know such a place, my dear?' The colonel tried to ignore his wife.

'No, no, madam. *Scotland* Yard. In short, I am Chief Inspector Whipple of Scotland Yard.'

As Augustine and Whipple continued to confuse one another, I detected the wolfhound's unease as he finished the last of the mustard. The animal made strange noises from both ends of its impressive torso.

I could see HG had detected the dog's strange murmur-ings and increasingly agitated body movements. The dowa-ger's efforts to interject the conversation between two people clearly misunderstanding each other's position failed, so the inevitable happened.

The hound issued forth at both ends, yelped, and ran for the duck pond.

'Has someone died?' said Augustine, such was the smell that even the citrus fruit failed to disguise.

I noted HG had seen and heard enough. 'Someone *has* died, and I suggest, Inspector Whipple, that you, Rex and I proceed to the crime scene at pace.'

2

AN ANNOUNCEMENT

Ambrose Bagley remained much as we'd left him earlier in the day, except the phenomenon of rigour mortice now held the fellow in its tight grip.

In fact, the deceased might easily have been mistaken for an ironing board were it not for his brogue shoes, to which the dowager objected because a gentleman would never consider such a vulgar shade of tan.

Inspector Whipple assumed command of the crime scene as if marshalling his troops ready for action. First, he ordered his two constables to scour the immediate area for anything that might imply a connection to the victim. Then he asked HG to recount our finding of Ambrose.

It immediately struck me as surprising how well they got on. The dowager was dazzling in an almost luminescent green three-quarter pleated skirt in the latest fashion with a light jacket and snug-fitting cloche hat. HG's ensemble favoured sensible day shoes with sturdy Louis heels.

For Whipple's part, he continued to sweat in his light brown mackintosh raincoat and dark brown trilby. For a plainclothes policeman, his attire did not strike me as offering a high degree of anonymity. His tall frame and pale pallor gave the impression of a man suffering from seasickness, rather than the strong bearing one might expect of Scotland Yard's world-famous crime-solver.

'The sight of blood and corpses doesn't agree with the inspector's constitution,' HG later confided, which I thought bizarre, given his line of business.

At any rate, the pair got on like a house on fire with each challenging the other's view with close attention and respect.

'You see the poor fellow's expression? As if surprised and disappointed at the same time.'

Whipple rubbed his clean-shaven chin between a finger and thumb as he leant forward to test HG's assessment. 'Then you're suggesting the man knew his assailant? As for his disappointment, I think that natural given the outcome of what took place here.'

I pondered the Whipple's latter point. So far, discussion surrounded the nature of Ambrose's position and injuries and not how or why he came to be beside the lake. I put this point to him, who at first gave me a suspicious look.

'Are you sure I haven't nicked you for something recently? A burglary perhaps, or the taking of a motor vehicle?'

Thankfully, HG put a stop to his interrogation. 'Cease this silliness, Arthur. You know perfectly well that Rex conveyed you from the train station. That he now wears a day suit instead of a chauffeur's uniform does not disguise the fact that it's the same fellow.'

The inspector looked me up and down, peering at me through almost closed eyes. 'Rex – what sort of a name is that for a chap?'

I looked to HG for further support on the matter.

'It is enough for you to know I consider this young man as my apprentice. I'm tutoring him in the art of sleuthing, speaking of which, I take it we agree the murderer knew Ambrose Bagley?'

The dowager's explanation of my status immediately changed Whipple's countenance toward me. Instead of taking an unhealthy interest in the possibility I was a criminal, the man merely sniffed the air and ignored my presence after offering a final half-glance and sort of sucking sound.

'Yes, I'm satisfied the assailant knew his victim and given you and several others are here for the weekend, I think it safe to say that our murderer lurks among the colonel's houseguests.'

I suggested he gather everyone in the great hall to interview them one by one.

'I am not an invention of Agatha Christie's imagination a la Hercule Poirot, sir. I'm engaged in an official Scotland Yard investigation as opposed to an instalment in the *Weekly Times*.'

'Stop this at once, Whipple. Again, you play the fool for reasons I cannot fathom. As for his suggestion, I think it quite an innovation.'

Whipple glanced in my direction before commenting, 'Quite so, HG.'

Fascinated that the dowager allowed the chief inspector to also address her as HG, I observed the exchanges between a Scotland Yard thief-taker at the height of his powers and an aristocrat with an impeccable lineage, and the connection would continue to puzzle me for some time to come. For the time being, I settled for listening to HG persuade Whipple to adopt my strategy.

However, there was to be one more surprise as we left Ambrose to the care of the medical profession. HG asked

Whipple if he had the time. The inspector instinctively reached for his fob watch, tucked into a small pocket in his waistcoat and secured with a silver chain.

'Getting on for five o'clock.'

'Precisely as I thought,' replied HG, though I did not at first appreciate the significance of her enquiry. 'Let me ask you a question, Arthur. Do you know of any man worth his salt who does not own a fob watch?'

I clandestinely checked my own to confirm ownership as Whipple harrumphed. 'In my experience, men who do not own a fob watch are of the dubious sort and inherently untrustworthy.'

HG clapped her hands as she gazed at the corpse. 'Are we to conclude that fellow is a bounder, then?'

Drawn to the deceased's garish waistcoat, which was plain to see now the chap was as stiff as a board, I deduced the meaning of HG's enquiry. Ambrose wore no such accessory.

Whipple eyed this latest revelation with interest. 'Perhaps that's why he holds his left hand thus, as if reaching out to recover something. Perhaps the killer removed the fob watch without this fellow's permission. What an unpleasant fellow the culprit must be.'

'I agree, Arthur. As my ward suggested, we must now gather the assembly and put method into our investigations.'

————

THE GREAT HALL OF BIRCHAM MANOR WAS, like much of the manor, remodelled in the 1870s in the Neo-Gothic style. One might say the building served as a testimony to Augustus Welby Pugin, who could have been accused of getting carried away when he interior design of our noble Houses of Parliament.

Gone were any traces of Tudor magnificence or the gayety of dainty Georgian colour schemes. Now all was heavy burgundies and stained oak furniture, which gave the voluminous room more the look of a court room than state room. However, this fitted our bill perfectly as a procession of staff entered the room from one end and the gentry from the opposite elevation.

I stood to one side as Chief Inspector Whipple and the dowager took centre stage. In front of them sat two rows of chairs, adjacent but with a gap between them in the manner of church pews. Staff to the left and gentry to the right.

'I have summoned you here to begin my investigations into the heinous murder of one Ambrose Bagley, late of Knightsbridge and, I suspect, a guest in this grand house for the weekend.' Whipple cast his arms about as if empha- sising the immenseness of the manor.

A hand shot up from the midst of the servant section. 'That is correct, Inspector. The gentleman was to stay in the Chinese bedroom, although I don't suppose he'll need it now, will he?'

The dowager entered the fray. 'Is this the case, Colonel?'

I thought it weird that the retired military gentleman appeared not to be familiar with his guests for the weekend.

'I expect my son, Peregrine, asked the chap. You know what these young fellows are like.'

A pause ensued as the assembly waited for said son to respond. 'Oh, he's not here,' said the colonel, 'he'll be pressing flowers or whatever it is would-be botanists get up to.'

I noted Whipple shook his head, which I took as a

measure of the famed inspector's frustration at the slow pace of progress.

'Let me be clear with you all. My view is that the person who murdered Ambrose Bagley is in this room or pressing flowers.' A tidal wave of murmurs coursed along the rows of people present. 'In which case, no one is to leave the house or grounds without my express consent. Is that understood?' The inspector's eagle eye cast its predatory stare from one to the next, defying dissent of any sort.

The quiet sob of a female floated from the back of the room. At the doorway to the great room leaned Rowena Dosett, a well-known flapper who kept rooms at the Ritz Hotel. The small, slim lady, dressed in a pastel blue frock and matching Mary Jane pumps, dabbed her eyes with a lace handkerchief.

'Did you know the deceased, miss?'

Whipple's directness caused HG to gravitate toward the young woman, who failed to answer the chief inspector's question.

Fed up with waiting, Whipple dismissed all present by repeating his order that no one should leave the premises and that they should each expect an interview on the matter.

'I'll leave you to consider two matters,' he concluded. 'If you're the guilty party, it's in your own best interest that you come forward, for I shall find the culprit, make no mistake about that. Secondly, should you have any information about the murder, heard or saw anything you think might interest the police, then it's your duty in upholding His Majesty's peace that you speak to me confidentially.'

Shortly after, Whipple began interviewing the paid staff while the houseguests and their host retired to the morning room for tea and crumpets.

Such gatherings provided me with an astonishing insight into how HG went about her sleuthing. As I occupied myself with examining a portfolio of pressed flowers compiled by the colonel's son in a bay window seat of the delightfully presented morning room, the dowager directed the conversation in such a way as to benefit her investigation while doing nothing to undermine her great friend Arthur Whipple.

Although I was unable to hear all the conversation, the titbits I picked up, together with HG telling me all later, propelled our investigations into unchartered territory.

I here recall a flavour of the dowager's technique to elicit information of import.

Sitting close by Rowena Dosett, HG attempted to comfort the young lady. 'Did you know Ambrose well?' This was a term the dowager always deployed to great effect. Although spoken with a true heart and natural integrity, it did the trick in disarming the beneficiary.

'I loved him dearly and we were engaged.'

The announcement brought a gasp from one section of the room and derision from others.

'Why do you mock, young sir? You're Berty Blowers' sole offspring, are you not?' His lack of response did not go down well with HG. 'Speak, boy. Are you related to that rascal of a man or are you not? Come, speak up, man.'

The man smirked. 'I have that pleasure, Your Grace. And I did not smirk, at least not at the young lady. Ambrose deserves no better than he got. The man was a bounder and a cad.'

'Fredrick Blowers, you have no right to talk about my Ambrose like that. He was a perfect gentleman and particularly good at playing the saxophone, which I'm told is a most difficult instrument to master. What have you to show for your life to date? A failed Bolivian gold mine venture through which you ruined several perfectly respectable gentlemen, and an abiding habit of grinding your teeth?'

I noted the gentleman immediately stopped moving his lower jaw from side to side, which led me to believe he took Miss Dosett's accusation to heart. Perhaps the fellow wasn't so jaunty after all.

Unexpectedly, a second gentleman sallied forth. 'Ambrose was a decent sort, but not good enough for you, my darling Rowena.' The chap's protestation looked even stranger given the white trousers, pink and white striped boating jacket, and straw boater which, for some inexplicable reason, he failed to remove while indoors.

Miss Dosett's response paved the way for several additional avenues HG and I were to follow in pursuit of Ambrose's murderer. 'Dear Lemuel, I love you as a brother, but nothing more. We have talked about this so often since being presented at court. It is simply not to be, my loyal friend.'

'Then I shall kill myself, just as I...' But the man tailed off with a faraway look.

———

AFTER THE TENSE ATMOSPHERE OF THE MORNING ROOM, HG and I enjoyed a pleasant walk in the extensive grounds of the manor. From our vantage point, we could see house staff coming and going from the great hall as Whipple continued interviewing all persons on the premises.

'Are we to believe that young Lemuel Norris accosted Ambrose and we are, in fact, investigating a crime of passion?'

At first, I found the proposition attractive, but considered it too convenient that a young man should make a statement tantamount to an admission of murder. I expressed my concerns to HG, who appeared to be busy watching one of the ground staff.

'We should talk to the gardener. If in the grounds this morning, he may have heard or seen something.' By 'we' I knew HG meant me and made a mental note of the task. 'Now, we were discussing Lemuel, were we not? I suppose you may have a point that it's too convenient. Another way of looking at this is that the boy intentionally made himself look silly and, therefore, harmless when, in fact, he's our murderer. I call such people clever fools. It plays to their hand to be thought imbecilic. It allows them the time and space to complete whatever it is they're up to.'

I reflected on this point, eventually concluding such an approach may lead one to jump at one's own shadow in attempting to untangle real from imagined conspiracies.

Our deliberations ceased as Whipple appeared on the horizon. HG commented he looked like a man needing a friend, so we doubled back to greet him. His mood appeared dark as he removed his trilby and wiped a layer of perspiration from his brow.

'If one more person informs me what a nice place the manor is to work, and how kind the family are to their staff, I shall puke.'

HG questioned why he should see anything but truth in the matter.

Inspector Whipple said that if something sounds too good to be true, then it usually is too good to be true. He added that, 'No family is perfect, for this is how the Percival-Travers are being portrayed, and I don't buy it.'

The dowager held her counsel, which I at first thought strange, since HG was not a woman to hold back when something needed saying or doing. Eventually, she ceased opening and closing her parasol as a measure to abate midges and stuck the steel tip into the soft ground as if about to use it as a shooting stick. 'Far be it from me to cast aspersions. However, I understand young Peregrine likes to press more than flowers. In fact, he has quite a reputation for visiting the ladies in certain noble homes within our capital city.'

HG had given me another valuable lesson in her many skills as a sleuth of repute. Born in 1856, Her Grace, or the Honourable Miss Eleanor Fitzgibbons as she was then, grew up among the very highest of society and named Queen Victoria as a godmother figure. In later years, the queen retained HG as a close confidant. This position, combined with a good marriage, maintained that HG was able to open any door she wished to enter.

The dowager informs me she still enjoys extensive access to the very highest circles, after going through a rough patch between 1901 and 1910 when Queen Victoria's eldest son, Bertie, was king. 'A man of eccentric morals who had an even more eccentric chair-like construction made for him in Paris', was all she said on the matter.

However, HG conceded his great triumph in establishing the Entente Cordiale with the French in 1904, when relations soured between our two countries. 'He went to Paris with them virtually throwing rocks at him and came away a couple of weeks later with the French eating out of his hands.'

As I mused on the matter, I lost sight of HG and Whipple. Only the inspector's distinct growl alerted me to their location as he berated one of his constables for not being correctly turned out as a member of His Majesty's constabulary.

'Adjust your article, PC Willows, or you'll be walking in front of the commissioner's car with a red flag.'

I arrived in time to observe the hapless bobby repositioning the strap on his helmet so it rested on the cusp of, rather than under, his chin. Foolishly, I thought, the constable, who I took to be around my age, contested the matter.

'But sir, parliament repealed the Locomotive Act in 1896. The law no longer exists.'

Over the many years I would collaborate with Whipple, what followed was one of only perhaps three occasions I witnessed the inspector almost resort to physical violence.

'Young man,' started the inspector ominously, 'I am the law. If I say you'll walk in the road carrying a red flag before you, that's what you'll do. Do not think for one moment that your knowledge of the law impresses me. Showing off isn't something I admire in my officers. In fact, knowing too much may positively harm your career. So that you may reflect on matters, you'll now scout the entire estate for further evidence and report to me when completed. Now get out of my sight.'

'But sir, the cook says tea will be ready in an hour.'

'Then you'd better get a move on. Jenkins, you get back to the manor house and see what you can dig up from the younger servants.'

Though I felt sympathy for PC Willows, I couldn't help feeling he'd brought the wrath of Scotland Yard down on his own head. Conversely, PC Jenkins appeared pleased with the turn of events.

HG had waited patiently throughout the episode, something I took as a measure of her respect for the inspector. However, now she appeared restless. 'Let us get on. We must isolate the houseguests from one another and capture their recollection of events and their views of poor Ambrose.'

Entering the front door to the manor while ignoring the crotchety butler, we were presented with a scene of mayhem before us. Rushing down the grand staircase came Rowena Dosett in floods of tears, followed quickly by Lemuel Norris.

'What a terrible thing for you to say,' wailed the inconsolable Rowena.

'What did he say, I wonder,' mused HG as she whispered into my ear.

'I mean it; I'm glad he's dead,' replied Lemuel as he pursued his heart's desire into the butler's pantry.

3

SECRETS

On the direct instructions of HG, I slipped from an environment of comfort and entitlement to an underworld of toil. The dowager expected that the staff might reveal tantalising gossip relating to the tragic events of the previous day.

Previous experience of observing the contrast between the upstairs rooms of the great English country houses and those of the servants' environment prepared me well for the scene as I entered the kitchen.

The master of the house being in residence meant that the inside staff had to have finished their own meal by 6.30 pm, to ready themselves to finish preparations and serve dinner at 8.00 pm on the dot.

On this occasion, however, the kitchen staff looked markedly relaxed and a sense of genial bonhomie prevailed. I soon realised the solution to this puzzle lay in neither the butler nor housekeeper being present. Instead, the servants' table rested in the jovial arms of Doris Lovejoy.

Doris possessed that rare combination of authority and

kindness. Cross her in professional matters related to her kitchen or cooking and she would bring down the house upon the transgressor. Work hard and admit any mistakes and the cook might treat one as a wayward child requiring instruction.

Doris left me with one lasting impression that was unlike the typical characterisation of female cooks found in penny dreadful magazines, popular in some social circles. There they are often short, rotund with a liking for sherry.

No, Doris Lovejoy was a tall, slim, elegant woman with delicate long fingers and penetrating blue eyes. A woman who, I would hazard a guess, was early into her fifth decade. Presenting herself in a brilliant white starched apron and hat, Doris ruled her domain without equal.

As I took my allotted seat near the head of the table, commensurate with being a visitor, I glimpsed Mable Popkiss, assistant cook back at Drakeford Old Hall. HG had sent her ahead to assist Doris with the colonel's guests.

Invited to say Grace, I willingly obliged, keeping it short as I noticed several staff members looking at the shepherd's pie with ravenous eyes. Within a minute, plates filled, the gossip began.

Meanwhile, I satisfied myself making conversation with the cook by asking what delights she'd prepared for the colonel and his guests.

'Oxtail soup, then Beef Wellington followed by Eton Mess, which is the master's favourite,' Doris replied as she monitored the shepherd's pie to ensure each of the staff received their fair share.

'It appears a happy household,' I ventured. 'That is, apart from dreadful recent events.'

My combined question and statement elicited not more

than a sympathetic nod from the cook as she gave one footman a stern look for taking a third slice of freshly baked crusty bread.

Events then took their own course when one of the younger parlour maids exclaimed, 'I know, let's all play *Guess the Murderer!*'

I looked to Doris, expecting her to reprimand the youth.

Not so; instead she merely cautioned all present to be on their guard for the return of the butler or housekeeper. 'You know what they're like.'

A ripple of conspiratorial giggles swept the long pine table as staff looked one way then the other to check the coast was clear.

'Who's going first?' said the parlour maid.

'You are, Peggy. It's your idea.'

I watched the eager staff applaud as the young girl got to her feet, only for Doris to quietly reprimand them for making too much noise, which might, she warned, bring unwanted attention to their proceedings.

'I think that Lemuel Norris person did it, you know; biffed Mr Bagley and killed him and all that.'

Several staff members appeared to agree, given the vigorousness with which they nodded. 'I heard him say he'd kill himself if Miss Dosett wouldn't have him. My bet is he got rid of his rival.'

'What about Mr Blowers? I heard the butler tell the butcher what he'd overheard the man say about that Ambrose chap,' said another.

Then a young maid, who I took to be not yet fifteen, slowly stood, her cheeks flushed with nervousness. 'Well, that's nothing. I saw Mr Peregrine watching Miss Dosett on the landing. He didn't see me but was having a right old look. Scary if you ask me.'

I should explain that the maid identified Peregrine Percival-Travers, the colonel's son. Where no title exists, staff often refer to members of their employer's family by prefixing a first name with the relevant pronoun as a mark of respect.

The maid's revelation caused much murmuring among the staff as one debated with another on the relative guilt of each party mentioned.

'Well, that's nothing,' said the boot boy. 'I was having a fag with Stan this morning and he said he hated them all and good riddance.'

The room erupted into laughter as the boy, who I estimated to be no older than fourteen years, caught the cook's eye, who summoned him to her side. 'You are much too young to smoke, my lad, let alone gossip. Now, tell me, what else did Stan Price say?'

The staff clearly appreciated the cook's indulgence of the scrawny boy, whose hair appeared not to have seen a comb this side of Easter.

Unfortunately, before I gathered further intelligence, the room fell into an immediate stony silence, which I took to mean either the butler or housekeeper, or both, had returned.

The sound of a gruff voice behind me confirmed matters. 'To your duties immediately or we shall be late serving dinner. May I remind you that this house is never late serving dinner. Get to it.'

———

WHILE I HUDDLED WITH THE DOWAGER AS OTHER houseguests mingled for pre-dinner drinks, the drawing room took on a different guise as ladies' formal dresses shimmered in the light and men's formal attire lent an air of gilded authority.

HG listened carefully as I relayed the information gleaned from the servants' tea, in particular, mention of the gardener and the peculiar behaviour of Peregrine.

'We must track both down as a matter of urgency to see what they have to say for themselves,' she said, all the while watching the other guests.

On one occasion I asked the dowager about her habit of people watching. From this enquiry, I learned a valuable lesson in reading a person's body language, particularly when the individual is under stress. HG maintained that facial twitches, a hand momentarily covering the mouth while speaking or, among other signs, a person averting their eyes under interrogation, might point to guilt.

As I began my own observations, HG drew my attention to Fredrick Blowers, who appeared to be glaring at Lemuel Norris, who never took his eyes off Rowena Dosett.

'Notice that Fredrick does not look at the young lady, only Lemuel. What does this tell you?'

Aware of being tested by my tutor, I redoubled my observations to pick up subtle clues that might give away the man's intention.

After several seconds and a further prompt form the dowager, I observed that the former acted as an animal at the top of the food chain thinking about their next meal, whereas the latter, Lemuel, looked pitiful as he watched Rowena giggle in conversation with Watkins-Simms the elder as though having not a care in the world.

HG rebuked me for missing one vital clue. While accepting my assessment of Frederick Blowers, she required that I re-evaluate my deductions concerning Lemuel. 'Do you not see the hatred in his eyes, his stiff posture, as if a coiled spring?'

On closer inspection, I withdrew my earlier comments on the fellow and apologised to HG for missing several vital components of the man's demeanour.

'Worry not,' came the dowager's reply. 'Take this as a lesson in questioning what you think you're observing with what is actually taking place.'

I now observed a man rebuffed by the love of his life and scorned by his contemporaries. What might such a man be capable of? HG had long held the view that all men, and women, were capable of the greatest feats of strength, brutality and deceit under certain circumstances.

Could it be that beneath Lemuel's timid appearance hid a monster capable of murder? After all, perhaps killing becomes easier and if so, might Lemuel now have his sights on Watkins-Simms the elder, who at this very moment beguiled the innocence of the young lady?

As I conveyed my new outlook on the situation, HG congratulated me for a willingness to admit my failings and learn from them. A lesson I learned repeatedly over the many years our association continued.

HG's attention once again wandered as Whipple surreptitiously entered the drawing room. 'Oh dear,' sighed the dowager.

Whipple, now shorn of his day suit, collar and tie, appeared in a dinner suit at least two sizes too big for the man. 'I swear the butler did it on purpose to humiliate me,' spat the inspector as he hid his baggy frame behind HG in the large bay window recess of the fine room.

'Not at all, Arthur. You look a picture of elegance, does he not, Rex?'

How was I to respond? Perhaps lie and give the fellow some temporary comfort, or be truthful, reinforcing all that Whipple already believed the case to be? 'You represent all that's fine about an English gentleman, Chief Inspector,' I replied, before averting my eyes for fear of giving the game away.

Thankfully, further embarrassment was stayed by the butler banging the dinner gong precisely on the stroke of eight.

'I take it you don't require a second hot meal in the space of ninety minutes, so I suggest you catch up with Mable to see if she has gleaned anything from her colleagues besides that you deduced in the servants' hall.'

With that, the dowager hitched up her skirts a little to make perambulation easier and avoid a tangle with her white satin slipper shoes. Whipple thrust both hands into his pockets to keep the oversized trousers loaned by the colonel from descending to the ground and hid behind HG's skirts.

Back in the kitchen, things were quiet as the cook put the finishing touches to the Eton Mess and placed it in the dining room servery via a dumbwaiter in the far corner of the sizeable kitchen.

'Have you seen Mable?' I asked.

Doris smiled and pointed to the small courtyard. Thinking she'd spotted my affection for Mable, I hid my blushes and proceeded at pace across the stone floor and exited a small scullery that led off the kitchen via a heavy wooden door.

———

'WHAT ARE YOU DOING SNEAKING UP ON A GIRL LIKE THAT, REX Sutherland? Call yourself a gentleman?'

After being mildly amused at catching Mable unawares, I quickly realised she did not think the matter funny in the slightest.

It took some abject apologies and cajoling for me to get back into the excellent books of a woman I was most fond of, though I have to say I suspected Mable of laying it on thick to maximise my embarrassment.

'Shush,' I said, guarding her against using my surname in public.

Having glanced around the deserted courtyard and giving me a most curious look, her only response was, 'So the dowager hasn't told them who you really are, then?'

The matter was not something I wished discussed, so I changed the subject, which Mable seemed not to object to, save for a shake of her head and a certain tutting noise made too loudly for my comfort.

'Aside from what the staff said at tea, have you any gossip for me?' My question seemed at first to shock Mable, before a rakish smile spread across her wonderful features.

'Funny you should ask that, but you know why the butler and housekeeper were absent from the servants' hall, don't you?'

I have to say one of my pet hates revolves around a person answering a question with a different question. Tempted to say that if I knew I wouldn't be asking, I tempered the urge to save annoying the wonderful Mable for the second time in as many minutes.

'No, I don't,' I replied, giving Mable the perfect opportunity to share her secret.

'They are having an affair. Yes, it's true. Doris Lovejoy said so.'

Knowing the cook's word to be unimpeachable, I pressed my enquiry. It seemed the two had known each other for some time, though the housekeeper had only recently joined the family after many years' service in a big house somewhere in Northumberland.

'And cook says she didn't get a reference, so the butler fixed it so he did the interview.'

My astonishment that a butler might conduct such an interview instead of the lady of the house clearly showed by my reaction.

'Cook says Augustine Percival-Travers is three sheets to the wind and leaves such matters to the man so she can concentrate on... well, no one seems to know what she concentrates on.'

'Anything else?' I responded, hoping to escape further detail of the curmudgeonly butler and surly housekeeper's nocturnal meanderings.

'Well,' replied Mable. 'That Peregrine chap watches people. He never talks to them, just watches, like.'

I thought a pattern emerging concerning several of the houseguests and family members. However, I could make neither head nor tail of what these trends pointed to.

For the remaining few minutes of peace I had with Mable, we talked about what we might like to do in the future and lamented the burden we each bore concerning our first or surname.

'I shall be glad to marry. Who wants a surname like Popkiss? I hate it and want rid of the thing.'

I enquired if the possession of a decent last name was all a likely candidate need offer. Mable took several seconds before adding that the man must be kind, worldly-wise and not mind too much about her passion for crocheting.

Before I had the chance to offer my own credentials, a breathless groundsman burst into the courtyard.

'Thank the Lord someone's here. There is a body of a man in the lake.'

4

A RACING CERT

I stood outside the closed double-doors of the dining room, contemplating how to enter. Certain that the inspector and HG should wish to know at their early conve-nience a second tragedy had taken place, I decided my only course of action lay in keeping my eyes fixed on the dowa-ger, whom I knew would alert to my presence immediately.

And so it turned out to be. Joining the glittering assembly as quietly as possible, I was, at first, disappointed to see that the dowager sat immediately to the colonel's right at the far end of the long Regency dining table.

Taken by the splendid array of solid silver candlesticks, decorative pieces and flower arrangements that lined the centre of the enormous table, I also felt upwards of a dozen elegantly dressed individuals looking at me with curiosity, along with the inverted snobbery exhibited by the servants waiting at table.

'Who disturbs enjoyment of my Eton Mess? Oh, it's that Rex fellow. Eleanor, why does he intrude upon us?'

Pleasingly, HG ignored her host and leant back in her

chair, ready to receive my urgent communication. Upon my whispering into her left ear, HG took only two seconds to show the seriousness of the situation to Inspector Whipple. 'Come,' she said in a quiet but direct tone. 'We must away to the lake.'

Whipple looked far from pleased as he gave his Eton Mess a last, lingering look, as friends might do on parting, before getting to his feet and following the dowager and me out of the grand room.

'What occurs?' asked the colonel in a grumpy tone. Quick as a flash, the dowager retorted that reports of a burglar at her Drakeford residence had come to her attention and required an immediate response from Scotland Yard.

Some may view HG's capacity to tell untruths with such sincerity to be at odds with a person known to be of the highest moral character. However, I took her course of action as an honourable attempt to spare the anxiety of all present and allow the colonel to finish his Eton Mess with a measure of satisfaction.

As we neared the lake, I marvelled at the inspector's focus on the job in hand, despite continuing efforts to stop his oversized trousers descending.

Several outdoor staff gathered in a huddle as we arrived at the water's edge, with one pointing to the figure in the middle of the lake, the fading light making it difficult to make out any solid edges.

HG immediately ordered a nearby small rowing boat be launched and gently berated the fellows for not having done so earlier. Galvanised by the dowager's authoritative tone, two men seized the craft and set off for the only bit of the solitary figure that remained above the water: an outreached arm pointing to the sky.

Inspector Whipple commented that the stricken fellow resembled the Lady of the Lake, minus Excalibur.

'A most astute observation,' replied HG before adding her own aside. 'To misquote the great Oscar Wilde, "To lose one houseguest may be regarded as a misfortune; to lose two looks like bad manners."' Whipple nodded in appreciation of HG's remembrance of such a brilliant literary figure.

Out on the lake, the two boatmen rowed with vigour to reach their quarry before all signs of the unfortunate person disappeared into the depth, even though the lake was unlikely to be over six feet deep. The recovery team performed sterling work as they grabbed at the few remaining fingers still above the surface.

Slowly, the team pulled up the victim. One could tell the more of the fellow that appeared, the heavier the work became. As usual, HG busied herself looking all around to detect anything out of place that might give a clue to what had taken place.

'Likely as not to be an unfortunate accident, or a case of a gentleman wishing to end it all,' offered the chief inspector. HG queried how the fellow ended up in the middle of a large lake without the benefit of a boat, since she had directed staff to use the only vessel in sight.

My view revolved around the chap either wading into the water as if paddling at Bognor Regis, or swimming to his chosen spot before giving up the ghost.

Whipple argued for my cause, though thought swimming out by far the more likely course of action since the water's edge plunged steeply from the bank.

By the time the small boat reached its reception party, the light had almost gone. Several men helped lift the poor wretch from the boat and onto the leaf-scattered dry earth.

I deduced the man to be in his late twenties or early thirties, although his pallor and wrinkly appearance may have prematurely aged the unfortunate chap.

Although giving all the signs of being smartly attired, closer inspection showed that he had a hole in the sole of his right shoe, stuffed with newspaper to keep the worst of the weather out.

Also, his trousers bore all the hallmarks of being shortened in a most unprofessional manner. No gentleman of means would wear the new-fangled 'off the shelf' attire, instead favouring London's Savile Row for expert, made to measure tailoring.

Finally, I observed that the poor chap's hair was longer than the fashion of the day for a fellow about town. More than this, an uneven edge to certain areas showed a self-inflicted fashion faux pas instead of the employment of a gentleman's barber.

The drowned man rested motionless with HG and Whipple standing on opposite sides of the damp figure, exchanging hypotheses on how the man came to be on the colonel's estate.

At length, he knelt by the body and began a diligent search through the man's pockets. 'I suppose we'd better establish who the fellow is.'

'Odd,' said the inspector as he completed his search of the drowned man. 'Not a scrap to identify the chap, nor does he have a penny-piece to his name.'

I mused that his wallet may have fallen from his jacket when in the water. Whipple sighed and lamented he'd have to arrange a search to check if that was the case.

As Whipple carried out a last check for anything that might inform as to the man's identity, I noticed a mark behind the fellow's right ear and enquired if this might be pertinent.

'You may have a point,' he replied. 'Two men dead within hours of each other in practically the same location is no mere coincidence.'

HG asked that I inspect the deceased's wrists. I knew at once what the dowager thought. Might the man have had his hands tied by rope? Close inspection showed his hands to be free of rope, yet the backs of both showed heavy bruising. His right hand also had a nasty cut to its outside edge, as if made with a sharp knife.

Whipple dismissed my findings, saying perhaps the man struggled to launch the rowing boat, bruising and cutting his hands in the process before abandoning his plan.

HG tutted, which informed Whipple and me that she dissented. 'Or someone held his hands tight while they rowed him out to meet his fate. Perhaps they cut his hand to encourage the poor fellow to comply?'

'But we have no evidence to suggest the victim was still alive when taken onto the water, if indeed that is what happened,' responded Whipple. 'He may have already been dead and someone wished simply to dump his body.' He turned to one of two constables. 'Get the doctor down here and ask that he gives me his preliminary findings as soon as possible. I shall be in the snooker room.'

Now alone with the forlorn fellow, all others having either returned to their duties or retired to leisure activities with the other guests, I ponded how desperate a person would have to be to take their own life, if that's what the fellow had done.

It put me in mind of my father who, at various times in his life had, for want of a better description, fallen into a pit of despair at our situation. I knew instinctively as a child how difficult he found raising me, Mother having died before my fifth birthday.

There were, of course, good times when money appeared more abundant than at other times, but overall, his finances were precarious as we moved from one lodging house to the next.

It was while recalling my early childhood that I glanced a scrap of dry paper. Thinking it abnormal that such a thing should rest on the surface of the lawn given the number of garden staff the colonel employed, I recovered it.

'2.30 Earl Derby. Haydock.'

I was at first confused. How might such a fellow as lay before me secure a meeting with the earl?

Also, if this was the case, how might he record the wrong location, since the family seat of the earldom is in Knowsley and not Haydock? Then it came to me. The note did not refer to the earl but a racecourse named after its geographic location.

My thoughts interrupted by the doctor and two members of the outside staff, I placed the scrap of paper into my wallet and headed back to the manor.

———

IT SEEMED MORE THAN A LITTLE ODD TO ENTER A GAMES ROOM to see life going on as normal when an unexplained death had occurred on that morning. Of course, I knew the English upper classes to be eccentric in their ways, but I expected at least a modicum of solemnity.

I responded to Whipple's gesture that I should join him at the billiard score board. Showing him the scrap of paper I'd recovered, I awaited his response with interest. The inspector, having quietly reprimanded me for contaminating possible police evidence, glanced at the item without showing much interest. I took this as a sign he wished not to alert those present to what had taken place at the lake.

'We must assume this has a bearing on recent events, even if at this moment I know not what it might be.'

He flicked a finger to indicate I should conceal the scrap about my person, before guiding me to one of the rich red leather bench seats that lined each wall of the oblong-shaped room in order to blend in more naturally with our surroundings and company. Whipple reminisced about his childhood, brought on by the luxurious surroundings we presently found ourselves in.

'Do you know,' he began. 'I lived in a two-up, two-down terraced house in Lambeth with my parents and three brothers and sisters. The lavatory was in a communal block in the back yard, as was the water tap.' He shook his head as he glanced at the rich embossed leather wallcoverings and bright electric lights.

'We had a gas lamp in the living room and that was it. For the rest, we used oil lamps or, when there wasn't enough money, tallow candles. You wouldn't believe how much muck and stink tallow candles give off, young man.'

I had significant experience of such candles but decided not to inform the inspector in case I stole his thunder.

Before Whipple could continue with his life story, the colonel called us all to attention. 'Gentlemen, shall we go through to the ladies or they will think we're lost? I know several of their number who might rejoice at such an outcome.'

What I suspected was the colonel's standard joke on such occasions raised little laughter. Instead, the group of well-turned-out gentlemen made their way through a haze of cigar smoke out into the corridor, off which the drawing room lay.

On entering, inspector Whipple announced the tragic death of a second person. A hushed silence morphed into a general murmur as the gathering took in the awful news.

'I wish to reassure you that Scotland Yard won't allow these two deaths to go unaccounted for. Just now we have no sign the second fellow met his end other than because of an accident. I shall continue my diligent enquiries into both deaths.'

To his credit, the colonel commiserated the death of both men.

His wife, Augustine, was a little less morose. 'Two bodies in one day; that must be a record,' she said, before picking up a copy of *Vogue* and devoting her attention to the latest fashions.

HG gave me a nudge. 'She plays the fool. It is unlikely to be the last occasion you witness such nonsense from that person this weekend.'

From the far side of the room, Watkins-Simms the elder offered several sympathetic words for the deceased, only for his twin brother, Watkins-Simms the younger, to pour scorn on his older brother's remarks.

'My twin has always been too soft on such matters. You would've thought being eleven minutes older than me would bring with it a certain wisdom and maturity. Not so. My view is that the fellow that drowned was probably trespassing, something he will most assuredly not do again.'

Again, HG nudged my arm. 'And so, the stakes increase between those two, mark my words.'

'World is going to the dogs with all these trespassers about the place,' said the colonel, which at least had the effect of breaking what had turned into an awkward silence after the tense exchange between the twin brothers.

Picking up on the theme, HG suggested that the

drowned man was well-dressed and might, therefore, have been on his way to join them for the weekend. I thought this to be plausible, except for the poor state of the man's clothes, despite what the dowager had said. 'Has anyone who was invited not yet arrived?' asked HG.

The colonel shrugged his shoulders and looked at his wife. As she put down her copy of *Vogue*, Augustine's facial expression showed bemusement. At this point, the butler, who was standing beside his mistress' chair, holding a silver tray on which reposed the whisky decanter and two unused glasses, bent forward and whispered something into her ear.

Still appearing baffled by the turn of events, Augustine announced, 'It seems we are missing a Mr Morgan Prescott. I understand the gentleman discovered deceased this morning asked that Mr Prescott be invited.'

5

ANYONE FOR TENNIS?

Having slept soundly, despite the traumas of the previous day, I entered the dining room of Bircham Manor in good spirits as I observed the comings and goings of the great and good of England.

Although an elegant ormolu clock on the Adams-style fireplace showed nine thirty on this sunny Saturday morning, my fellow diners appeared much the worse for wear from a late Friday night playing cribbage and, perhaps, imbibing too much whisky and port.

I realised except for HG and Inspector Whipple, few guests had any understanding that the working day for most of His Majesty's subjects had started some three to four hours ago.

'Good morning, Rex,' said HG brightly as she ate her boiled egg and crustless toast fingers with grace.

The inspector merely grunted to acknowledge my presence as he continued to devour a heaped plate of Cumberland sausage, kedgeree and, of all things, baked beans.

'Don't ask,' said the dowager as we exchanged an amused glance.

After a second cup of Twinings Breakfast Blend tea and picking remnants of smoked haddock from between his teeth, he mused the possibility that a multiple murderer lurked within our number. 'We must speak to that strange butler fellow again. What's his name? Oh, yes, Lomas. He has some explaining to do regarding Morgan Prescott's invitation. If nothing else, it proves he had contact with our first victim, the unfortunate Ambrose Bagley.'

The dowager appeared impressed at the Whipple's decisiveness. 'There's clearly something to be said for kedgeree, although I cannot stand the stuff myself.'

Her remark appeared to make little impression on the inspector as he eyed the one remaining roundel of Cumberland sausage on the buffet table to his right. However, before he could get to his feet, the inspector lost his prize to Watkins-Simms the elder. 'I see why his younger brother has issues with that man,' grumbled Whipple as he slouched back into his chair and glowered at the victor.

Fortunately, Whipple had little time to dwell on his loss as the colonel entered the room and called all to attention. 'Don't forget, everyone, the tennis tournament will begin at eleven, followed by a light picnic by the Japanese teahouse. I trust everyone has brought relevant attire. If not, have a word with one of the staff and they will sort you out.'

I watched Whipple wince at mention of being provided with clothing.

Before our host could make his escape, HG collard him. 'Dear Colonel. May we make use of the library to interview certain persons?' The dowager brought a hush to the room as each guest looked at their near neighbour with suspicion.

'Ah, I see, so you may catch your murderer, or perhaps, murderers.' The colonel laughed at his ill-timed joke. 'Yes, yes, of course. Inform Lomas whom you wish to interview, and he will see them delivered to you.' His eyes lifted to the dour butler, who stood statue-like, guarding the whisky decanter. The butler offered the merest nod in recognition of his employer's instruction.

'There's something different about that fellow, you know,' commented the inspector.

'Who, the colonel or the butler?' responded HG.

'Come to think of it, both,' retorted Whipple before making a break for the two fried eggs that remained in a silver tray heated with a small paraffin burner.

HG remarked to me she thought the detective's impoverished upbringing made him hate the thought of nutritious food going to waste. I well understood the sentiment from one or two tight spots I remembered as a child. However, the adult in me concluded Whipple's excessive morning appetite might deprive the downstairs staff of a little extra protein.

As the inspector re-took his seat, tucked his napkin into his collar and coveted his new acquisitions as if they were the crown jewels, HG's patience frayed. 'We must get a move on, Arthur. There is no time to lose. I take it we shall see Peregrine first?'

Whipple shook his head as he cut each egg into two and ate all four segments within thirty seconds. 'No, I want to see what the inscrutable Lomas has to say for himself. He adopts the posture of running this house; let us see if the man's loftiness trips him up.'

Whipple called over the butler as if summoning his bill in a provincial restaurant, a gesture Lomas did not appear to warm to. The unsmiling servant intertwined his white-gloved fingers as if preparing for a bare-knuckled fight and approached at the speed of a sloth with sore bunions.

'Sir?' he said with a certain edge that reminded me of a

maths teacher I once endured, and who specialised in treating his charges as if we were devoid of all sense.

'In the library in ten minutes if you don't mind.' The inspector paused for a moment before completing his instruction. 'Or even if you do mind for that matter.'

'Whom shall I summon first, Chief Inspector Whipple?' asked the butler as he sniffed the air.

'You, my man. We shall begin with you. So, until then, you may go.' Giving Lomas no time to discuss the matter further, Whipple got to his feet. 'A quick turn about the terrace before we start, I think.'

As our party made to leave, Dr Griffiths entered the now deserted room. 'Glad I've caught you,' he said without glancing at the buffet table. 'I've completed my initial report on both bodies and thought you might be interested in my findings?'

HG gestured for the doctor to take a seat. 'Tea?' she asked, which Griffiths turned down with grace.

'Thank you, but no. I have much to do this morning. Let us hope that Mr Prescott's post-mortem reveals a clear cause of death, if only to allow his family at least a measure of closure. As for Ambrose Bagley, he died because of a strike from a narrow object approximately one inch in width.'

This additional information left us baffled. 'What might have caused such an injury?' enquired HG.

The doctor was less forthcoming this time, stating that pending post-mortems on both men, he could not say for definite whether Prescott had ingested any water or died before being placed in the lake. Nor could he confirm what object caused Ambrose Bagley to depart this world.

THE LIBRARY, ON THE SOUTHERN ELEVATION OF THE MANOR, benefited from natural light flooding in from three large windows, each of which stood almost floor to ceiling. A heady mixture of leather and bound paper permeated a room that measured some twenty feet wide by thirty feet long.

Shelf upon shelf of precisely aligned books filled three walls, though I suspect that like many such families, the Percival-Travers purchased their inventory by the yard rather than for any academic or literary purposes.

Hardly had we been in the room for two minutes when the butler, Lomas, gave a single knock from a gloved hand and entered. The inspector directed the smartly dressed servant to a chair that he'd quicky positioned to face three others, with six feet between the opposing furniture.

Lomas sat, back ramrod straight, and awaited our first question. Whipple began by enquiring how the butler knew Ambrose Bagley had requested a room for Morgan Prescott, especially since the former passed away before setting foot in the manor.

HG leant forward a few inches, which I took to be a sign the dowager hoped to detect something of interest from the butler's body language and other non-verbal communications.

Keen to learn from my tutor, I also studied Lomas. The man's facial features bore all the hallmarks of a competent poker player. He gave nothing away. His eyes remained fixed and unblinking on the inspector, who toyed with a stubby pencil as he spoke.

'I cannot recall, Inspector,' was the butler's initial response.

Whipple, seemingly unperturbed, got to his feet and slowly walked around the butler's chair, keeping approximately four feet between them. This forced Lomas to spin his head to such an acute degree that it seemed impossible the surly man could recover from the endeavour.

'Don't give me that guff. I know your sort. All calm on the outside but panicking inside at the thought of being caught out. Now you listen to me. You tell me what you know or I'll have you in a cell before the sun sets. Do you get me, sir?' Whipple's emphasis on the word 'sir' exited the inspector's mouth with a certain menace, causing Lomas to blink rapidly.

HG leant into me and whispered, 'He knows something.'

The inspector clearly felt the same as he pressed the butler, who developed several beads of perspiration on his deeply furrowed brow.

'A telephone call. He rang me.'

I could see the inspector's renewed interest as he launched a salvo of questions in quick-fire fashion. How did Lomas know the man's name? How did Bagley address him? What time did he say they were to arrive?

The speed and directness of the inspector's verbal assault undid the butler as he mopped his damp brow with the white gloves he'd removed from his shaking hands.

'I... err, well.'

'Answer, man.'

'Mr Lomas... he called me Mr Lomas,' spluttered the butler. 'The gentleman said they were to arrive separately by train. He by 9.30 am yesterday and Mr Prescott shortly after ten forty-five.'

The late morning arrival struck a chord with me, although for what reason I could not fathom.

Whipple's interrogation concluded as quickly as it had begun. 'You may go now, and say nothing of the last ten minutes to anyone, do you understand? Now, locate and send in Miss Dosett.'

The inspector's habit of issuing multiple commands seemingly unconnected to one another was, I thought, a powerful tactic in throwing one's quarry off guard.

Over the course of the few minutes it took for the young lady to arrive, we three discussed the butler's performance and responses. Our consensus was that he had received a phone call. Whether the caller was Ambrose Bagley we thought entirely a different matter.

'Do come in,' said HG as she stood to greet a broken-hearted Rowena Dosett and guide the crying young lady to her seat. 'We have no wish to prolong our meeting more than strictly necessary to spare your pain, but can you tell us about Ambrose and if you knew of anyone who might wish to harm him?'

Rowena cried almost uncontrollably on hearing HG's sensitively spoken enquiry. Miss Dosett lamented Mr Bagley was the kindest, most civil and generous man it was possible for a lady to meet. 'I know of no one who might wish to harm him. Ambrose was universally loved.'

At this point, the young woman became inconsolable for what seemed like an age. HG quicky took charge by shooing Whipple and me out while she calmed the situation. It was a full ten minutes before the door opened again, this time not to invite us men back in but allow the lady to escape her ordeal.

As we reclaimed the library, having asked the butler to bring Lemuel Norris to us, HG shared the conversation she'd had with Rowena. 'That girl hinted that she'd seen Ambrose and Lemuel arguing over her two weeks previous while at a weekend party in Brighton.'

This information did not surprise us, given what we'd

witnessed Norris say about the deceased previously. When the man appeared before us, our line of interrogation sprang into action.

This time HG played the tough policeman. 'I can't imagine,' the dowager began, 'anyone failing to point a finger at you for the death of Ambrose Bagley. We all heard how you spoke of the dead man. What have you to say for yourself?'

The question appeared to flummox the fellow as he sat with his legs and arms crossed, staring blankly at the rich Persian carpet.

'Look at me,' barked the dowager.

Slowly, the man engaged HG's stern glare. 'I liked Ambrose and wished him no ill will. I'm devastated that he's dead.'

HG was having none of it. 'Come now, you are, or were, an ardent rival for a certain young lady's hand, were you not?'

The verbal onslaught illuminated a side of the dowager I had not before experienced, and I was glad Lemuel Norris sat opposite her and not I.

'Rowena loves me, not Ambrose. She showed as much to me. I shall bring nothing but joy and happiness to our union and have the funds to do so. What might Ambrose offer? A modest house in Knightsbridge and a Maid of All Works for company?'

The dowager didn't let up. 'Then why threaten to kill yourself if the girl failed to return your affection? Remember, we heard you saying – how did you put it? "Just like I did Ambrose?"'

I found Lemuel's calm response a revelation. 'I did not mention Ambrose's name,' he said, which I considered too calm and collected by half, given how agitated he appeared during his argument with Miss Dosett.

Whipple re-entered the game. 'Listen, I've come across this situation many times during my long career. A beautiful girl says she loves a man, another man, a love rival, you might say, and her betrothed becomes jealous. He attempts to reason with his rival, things get out of hand... then it happens. A pure accident born out of passion. That's what happened, wasn't it, Lemuel?'

I now understood how clever the partnership between HG and the inspector was. They complimented each other beautifully. One appearing aggressive, the other the very definition of reasonableness.

'I'll say only this, Chief Inspector; I love Rowena Dosett with every fibre of my being and would do anything to make her happy. However, I did not kill poor Ambrose. In fact, I had not seen the fellow for three months before this weekend.'

In an unwelcome development, the butler opened the heavy oak-panelled door to reveal his employer in a full set of gleaming white sportswear, which did little to show off his portly frame to best advantage.

'Come, come. No more of this interrogation business; your murderer can wait for tennis.'

———

LOCATED FIVE HUNDRED FEET FROM THE HOUSE, THE colonel's tennis court would not have looked out of place at the All England Lawn Tennis and Croquet Club in Wimbledon.

The full-sized court hid its stunning facilities from the surrounding grounds of the Manor by tall hedging and topiary clipped into the shapes of various animals. At one end, sufficiently far back to avoid the full impact of a stray tennis ball, stood a majestic open-fronted timber pavilion from where spectators might observe match play.

However, the pleasant surroundings did nothing to assuage the inspector's ire at his investigations being once more interrupted by the leisured class.

As we settled into our deckchairs and accepted a soothing glass of lemonade from one of the staff, the colonel announced that the Watkins-Simms twins were to be first on court in a match of mixed-doubles with their wives.

'Sparks will fly,' noted HG as she sipped her cooling refreshment.

Watkins-Simms the elder won the toss of a coin to serve first. Securely seated in his elevated position at the net, the colonel gave the all-clear for battle to begin.

From the outset, Simms the younger exhibited the more aggressive behaviour and within minutes both wives had withdrawn from the game. Observing their countenance, I could see they despised their spouses' public display of hostility.

HG beckoned both women, who appeared to get on well with each other, to join our party. Both busied themselves with anything other than watching the unfolding spectacle.

On court, Simms the younger acquitted himself well in parrying his older brother's penetrating serves. As younger fought elder and visa vera for control of the game, the intensity of their rivalry erupted as tennis rackets pummelled the ball with unrelenting ferocity. At length, the younger aimed a ball squarely at his older brother's head, sending the older brother reeling backwards into a collapsed heap on the cinder court surface.

A scream rang out from the elder's wife, diverting Whipple's obsession with observing the crowd for suspicious signs. Meanwhile, HG proceeded at pace to the playing area as the younger brother stomped from the court, blaspheming at his stricken brother as the man lay immobile, tennis racket still gripped tightly in his right hand.

Waiting for the inspector before joining the dowager, I attempted to give what succour I could to both wives as they looked on at unfolding events in horror.

'Quite a temper,' commented inspector Whipple as he pointed to Watkins-Simms the younger's rapid exit from proceedings.

Making no effort to defend her husband's actions, the younger man's wife explained his inability to accept his older brother inheriting their father's estate. This was despite the elder sibling giving his younger brother a generous allowance which, she said, he was under no obligation to do.

Our host watched events with mild disinterest as he checked the net for tautness.

Whipple bent over the slumped figure so that his open jacket almost obscured the victim's upper torso and head. After a few seconds, he stood, his flushed cheeks soon regaining their normal complexion after his exertions.

Observing the inspector's grave expression, one guest cried out, 'He's not moving; he's dead.'

6

THE GARDENER

Concern deepened as we watched Watkins-Simms the elder's prone body on the compacted cinder surface of the tennis court as Dr Griffiths approached.

'Let the dog see the bone, ladies and gentlemen,' said Griffiths as he knelt beside his patient. The furrows on his forehead relaxing heralded good news. The tennis player, although dreadfully concussed, was at least alive.

A cry of relief came from a little way behind me as Watkins-Simms' wife rushed by to comfort her husband, who now occupied a sitting position courtesy of the comforting help of Dr Griffiths.

'You must rest for the remainder of the day. My weekend to date is turning out to be quite hectic enough, without you taking a turn for the worse through not taking things easy,' said the doctor.

With the help of two members of staff and the miraculous appearance of a wheelchair, the stricken but conscious tennis player was wheeled back to the imposing house, followed by his concerned wife.

'Well, now that's settled,' began the colonel as he ceased

his interminable checks of the tennis court net, 'it's time for lunch. Over to the Japanese teahouse, everyone.'

It struck me as odd that within seconds of a grievously injured peer being wheeled off to bed rest, the others turned their full attention to cucumber sandwiches and home-made lemonade. Within thirty seconds, the tennis court and pavilion emptied as upwards of a dozen guests made their way to lunch, with a small retinue of staff bringing up the rear.

'Isn't this beautiful,' commented the dowager as we arrived at our destination. Here stood a delightfully ornate building in the Japanese style, which measured approximately eight feet square with cedar boarding to the bottom half and faux paper screens to its upper portion. As it stood on wooden stilts in tranquil water and shrubbery all around, one might reasonably assume we occupied the grounds of Tokyo's rural estates.

As several members of our party crossed an understated wooden bridge to gain access to the teahouse, the others, including, HG, Whipple and myself, elected to sit on the closely-mown grass and enjoy the sun as it reached its noon zenith.

The staff soon completed their task of ensuring all had sufficient food and drink before vanishing.

'What better place to undergo interrogation than an English garden in summer,' noted HG as inspector Whipple called for Mr Fredrick Blowers to join us while we sat some fifteen feet from the others to facilitate a measure of privacy.

Mr Blowers, he who had called our first victim, Ambrose, a 'bounder and a cad' the previous evening, adopted a casual appearance as he sauntered over to our position, hands firmly in pockets while whistling a tuneless tune.

'I've been expecting this, Inspector,' said the man as he sat on the dry grass and folded his white-trousered legs as if at school.

Having gone through the usual pleasantries, Whipple changed his tone in a heartbeat. 'Why did you hate Ambrose Bagley so much? Enough to kill. Speak, man, speak now.'

The onslaught appeared to ruffle Fredrick Blowers' feathers, and I knew it a tried and tested strategy from Whipple to put his quarry on the back foot.

Blowers reached for a cucumber sandwich, which I thought allowed him a few seconds to gather his wits. The man certainly did not appear to enjoy the small square of crustless bread which, judging by his facial expression, had stuck to the top of his mouth.

Whipple continued his relentless attack. 'We know a considerable amount about you, so out with it. Admit your guilt and tell me why you murdered that man.'

I wasn't sure if this amounted to a continuance of Whipple's well-rehearsed act, or if he possessed certain facts he was yet to reveal to the dowager and me.

'He cheated me, that's all,' blurted Blowers.

It seemed, according to the wretched man before us, that Ambrose Bagley had borrowed a substantial sum of money, some £2,000, to invest in a Bolivian railway venture that had come to nothing. 'He said the company had gone bust, and with it my money.'

HG, who had adopted the role of observer up to this point, raised a finger. 'Surely then, Mr Blowers, a perfect motive for murder. You know; if you couldn't get your cash, you'd get the man instead?'

By now Blowers had lost most of the colour from his cheeks. 'Then why am I telling you all this? I had no need to.

I could simply have said Ambrose and I argued over some trifle and left it at that.'

This I thought to be an interesting response. Was Blowers engaged in some form of game to throw us off the scent?

Inspector Whipple's eyes bore into Blowers, waiting, I imagined, for the man to break. Instead, Blowers held firm, a look of helplessness etched on his face.

'Do not leave the grounds,' barked Whipple as he hurriedly wrote something into a small notebook which he had a habit of pulling from the breast pocket of his jacket.

I thought the dampening of the pencil on his extended tongue and look of suspicion toward Blowers at regular intervals between scribblings to be most effective.

'That will do... for now,' said the inspector, dismissing Blowers with a wave of his hand as he continued to write.

HG caught my attention with a raised little finger-wag as she ate a fresh salmon sandwich. 'That fellow behind you. No, don't look. He reminds me of the chap I mentioned to you. Be so good and say hello to him. See what you can find out because he's been watching all that we've been up to.'

OBEYING MY INSTRUCTION, I GOT TO MY FEET AND MADE OFF in the opposite direction to where the dowager said the man stood. My strategy was to circle and catch him by surprise.

In the event, the man, one of the estate gardeners, also made off. It took me some time to track him down. Eventually, I came within ten feet of the fellow. Unfortunately, my stealthy approach worked all too well. As I tapped the man on his shoulder from behind, the burley fellow swung around, pulled back his arm and almost cuffed me one.

'What are you doing creeping up on me like that for?' he said, which I considered quite reasonable in the circumstances.

'Sorry, mate. I'm the Dowager Duchess of Drakeford's chauffer... and gardener, and handyman. You know what these aristocrats are like. I'm Rex. What's your name?'

I'm pleased to report that the fellow took my bait. 'Stan... Stan Price,' he said in a voice still tinged with suspicion. 'You don't look like a chauffeur to me,' he said.

Not quite knowing what such a person might look like, other than his uniform, I pondered offering a smart response but thought better of the idea. 'That's because of all the other things I do. Just look at my hands.' Fortunately for me, I had grazed several fingers picking up a heavy stone garden statue HG required moving at home some days earlier. My minor injuries provided the perfect stage prop.

Glancing at my open palms, Stan calmed down. 'You think you're hard done by – at least she looks a lady. My lot wouldn't give you the time of day if you were on fire. And all for seventy-five quid a year, plus a tied cottage. How much do you get?'

Thinking on my feet, I came up with a figure that might sound realistic to Stan. 'I do little better. Mine pays ninety-five a year, plus I get to sleep in the loft over the Rolls-Royce.'

Our shared financial position did the trick. Stan relaxed and leant on his spade as he gazed into the distance at nothing as far as I could see.

'Then yours are rubbish to work for?' My enquiry hit a rich seam as Stan moaned to me about his employers.

'To be fair, the colonel doesn't bother much. He spends most days fishing in his boat on the lake. And I suppose his missus is harmless. In fact, she's as mad as a box of frogs.

But the son, Peregrine, he's a piece of work, he is. Comes across as a daft flower collector, but you cross him, and you'll know about it. He can be a cruel one.'

Although I attempted several times to draw Stan out about what he meant, the man refused to elaborate. Instead, I changed tack by asking if he had a family and what he liked to do with any time off he got. Instead of helping the situation, my questions appeared to enrage the gardener.

'Nothing to tell. I've got work to do, so I'll be saying good afternoon to you.' With that, the man withdrew his spade form the hard ground, slung it over his shoulder, barely missing me, and stomped off toward a long herbaceous boarder that might not look out of place at Kew Gardens.

Admitting defeat, I began the pleasant walk back to HG and Inspector Whipple at the teahouse. Along the way, I noticed a figure in the distance, crouching on all fours. Intrigued, I set off in the stranger's general direction, taking care to remain clandestine by hugging a line of lime trees.

As I neared, I made out the unmistakable sight of Peregrine Percival-Travers, whom HG had previously described to me in great detail and who was the only son of our host. I assumed, given his apparent passion for flowers, that he was conducting research on a particular species of flora.

It was only when I stepped nearer that I noticed a small pair of field glasses. The man wasn't undertaking research, at least not of the botanical sort. No, although giving the appearance of inspecting the sword grass at close quarters, he was, in fact, taking a particular interest in Miss Rowena, whom I could barely make out at the lake's edge.

THE GENIAL CHATTERING OF FRIENDS ENJOYING A PLEASANT picnic filled the air as I re-joined the dowager and inspector Whipple at the teahouse.

'Did you get anything juicy?' enquired HG as I sat on the grass between my two lunch companions. I explained what had taken place, and in particular, the matter of Stan Price's sensitivity to family enquiries and my sighting of Peregrine.

'There's more we need to find out about that one,' said HG as she winked at me. 'I suppose you besmirched the aristocracy to find common ground between the two of you. If so, well done. In my experience, the paid staff are an invaluable source of information about their place of work and the family they work for. They know where all the skeletons lie.'

Inspector Whipple took interest in HG's reference to skeletons as he once more mopped his glinting brow.

I felt now was the time to slake my curiosity. 'Why don't you ever remove your jacket?'

The inspector hunched his shoulders before relaxing them again as if trying to dislodge something from between his shoulder blades. 'If you must know,' he started, 'I rushed down from London on Friday before changing. My shirt has a small tear in the back from catching and restraining a villain first thing on Friday. That said, it's the case that an English gentleman never takes his tie or jacket off in public.'

HG commented it was for this reason so many men of a certain position suffer from heatstroke in July and August.

Whipple appeared uninterested in the dowager's assessment as he kept a close eye on the comings and goings of the colonel's houseguests.

'Have none of them a job of work to do?' he said.

This brought a not entirely unexpected response from HG. 'Your deduction is, as usual, flawless, Arthur. I imagine they're unemployable since, in my experience, the average IQ of the leisured class falls south of a bluebottle in a glass jar not knowing quite what stalls its progress.

I thought HG's opinion incisive and pertinent, as did Whipple, as evidenced by his response. 'Present company excepted, of course.'

HG was generous enough to enter the spirit of things by poking the inspector with her open parasol and saying, 'Good answer, Arthur; you're learning. Rex, take note.'

At that point, Augustine Percival-Travers approached to enquire what we found so amusing.

'Intelligence, Augustine, we spoke of human intelligence.'

Our host replied that, 'Intelligence is a stranger to me and one I find best avoided, since I believe it leads to severe headaches.' Without further comment, Augustine sauntered off into the distance without looking back.

I noted inspector Whipple shared my bafflement, which HG clearly found amusing. 'Don't be fooled by that little performance. Augustine has one of the sharpest minds I know. It merely serves her purpose to keep it hidden from view. Believe it or not, she worked in Whitehall during the war. Very hush-hush.'

7

A PRESSING INTERVIEW

With so much happening over the past twenty-four hours, I took a turn by the lake. As I passed through a thick line of elm and ash trees that concealed the stretch of water from the Manor, I came across Inspector Whipple.

'I see you had the same idea as me.' Whipple's thoughtful gaze and strained body language told me everything I needed to know. 'You know... err, Rex, I deal with bad people every day of my working life, yet it still gets to me sometimes, you know, what one person can do to another, usually for the stupidest of reasons.' As he spoke, Whipple continued to stare across the still surface of the water and out across the borrowed view of the lush Kent countryside.

I lamented the truth of his words, but pointed out for every act of cruelty, there were many more examples of kindness people show to one another. 'Otherwise, what's the point of it all?' I offered.

I watched as the inspector rummaged around in his jacket pockets, eventually pulling out a small paper bag of confectionary.

'Everton Toffee Mints. So, you're a football fan?' My reference to the famous football club in Liverpool, nicknamed 'The Toffees' after the famous black and white striped sweet invented by a certain Molly Bushell in the 1760s, appeared to shock the inspector.

'Not on your life. I'm an Aston Villa man, but Everton mints are my favourite sweeties,' he replied before remembering his station in life. 'Now, do you want one or not? I don't care either way.' His outstretched arm remained in position long enough to select a mint before the paper bag disappeared into the seclusion of his jacket pocket.

The interlude did, however, give me the tiniest insight into a man who, I assumed for obvious reasons, needed to present a tough appearance. However, like most people, such behaviour concealed a gentler side, much like the dowager. This got me thinking and promoted a question to my waterside companion.

'How did you meet HG?'

'It's a big jump from football confectionary to a Lady of the Realm, isn't it?' he replied, sucking hard on his mint.

Rather than explaining my enquiry, I remained silent and watched Whipple as he considered his response.

He appeared to form his first word twice before actually speaking. Without turning his gaze from the water, Whipple finally spoke. 'Twenty years ago, I was a young detective sergeant who found himself, through a combination of circumstances, in charge of a murder case. You can imagine, the more senior officers and my contemporaries didn't take kindly to being directed by a young whippersnapper. There were plenty hoping – and expecting – that I'd fail, and I almost did.'

I suggested to the inspector that his change in fortune might have involved the dowager.

'We met purely by chance. HG was passing by in Hyde Park when she overheard the commissioner of police berating me at the lack of progress in finding the killer. I had set up an elaborate scheme to catch the man from a tip-off by one of my narks. The commissioner came along for the arrest, only for humiliation to follow when we almost arrested an innocent member of the public.'

Understanding where the inspector's tale was taking me, I supposed the dowager interceded on his behalf.

'Rather an understatement,' he replied. 'She tore into the commissioner who, naturally, she knew. Just as she knew Mr Akers-Douglas, home secretary. From then on, the commissioner let me be, and with HG's help, I got my man. He met his maker at Wormwood Scrubs three months later.'

Whipple said that he'd consulted with HG ever since and shared many successes, commenting that although tough and prepared to tell powerful people when they're wrong, she was and is one of the kindest persons he knew.

'You'll know about Horizons, of course?' For a moment I froze and acted as if oblivious to the reference. 'HG founded and still finances that children's home. London's East End can be a hard place. I doubt more than a handful of people know she's behind it, which, she tells me, is the way she prefers things.'

I then asked a question I regretted. 'You seem to speak fondly of children, Inspector. Have you any yourself?' Whipple's physical stature seemed to wither before my eyes. Realising I'd made a terrible mistake, but unaware why, I apologised.

'It's a long time ago now, so no need of an apology, but yes, I enjoy having children around me. It's as well, since HG roped me into helping at Horizons years ago. It helped.'

In deeper than I wanted to be and sensing the inspector wanted, almost needed, to talk, I asked why.

'My Jenny died having our first child. I lost them both, and...' The inspector's voice tailed off as he glanced back over the lake. 'Anyway,' he said after several seconds' quiet reflection. 'What about you?'

Uncomfortable at having to respond with the candour the inspector had given to my question, I thought about how best I should recount some painful memories. Thankfully, HG's appearance from the trees saved the day.

'I thought I'd find you two down here. And it's said that women are the ones that natter. Now come to the house. I've seen Peregrine and think we should speak to him.'

———

As we made our way back to the house, engaged in amiable chat, I realised someone was watching us. I said as much to my companions, and we each surreptitiously attempted to identify a strange figure on the treeline.

'I suppose,' began HG, 'that we have two candidates, based on their previous behaviour. I speak of Peregrine and the gardener.'

Our endeavours clearly alerted our observer as he slunk back into the safety and concealment of the trees, though I knew he continued to watch.

'Why do you suppose the man is so interested in our movements, Arthur?'

The inspector thought for a moment before responding, showing his concentration by rubbing his chin between forefinger and thumb. 'Perhaps we're not under his surveillance and it's this area he's interested in, an area we happen to occupy.'

I considered this a plausible line of thought, since both victims met their end in the same small area, albeit one on dry land and the other in water.

'Then you're suggesting the fellow is interested in what evidence may remain at the waterside. Of course, your men examined the area, did they not, Arthur?'

The inspector nodded. 'Yes, they did. However, the nature of the terrain down there means we might easily have missed something. Perhaps it's worth a second sweep.'

I speculated whether the man might be working on his own behalf, a murderer double-checking nothing remained, or if he interceded on behalf of another.

'You may well have a point,' said HG, to which Whipple concurred. 'Then, in that case, let us see what the colonel's son has to say for himself. It will also be worth having a further chat with your gardener friend, Rex.'

HG's reference to the gardener was once again not so much a comment as an instruction. The conundrum I faced was that our last meeting concluded on somewhat of a sour note.

As I contemplated how I might engineer a meeting with Stan Price, the colonel appeared as if out of nowhere to impede our progress.

'Are, there you are. May I ask how your investigations are going? Two dead bodies in one weekend will do nothing for my reputation as a civil host, you know.'

The inspector and I glanced at each other to silently agree we might leave any response to the dowager.

As I expected, HG oozed charm. 'Matters are progressing to our satisfaction, are they not, gentlemen?' This was our cue to nod in synchronicity. HG continued, 'We believe the drowning to be an accident, plain and simple.'

It was then that the inspector experienced an unusually severe cough, which startled everyone. As HG looked on with concern, I noticed a certain look between her and the inspector, which I took as a prompt to desist from giving further details.

The colonel gave Whipple a confused look as, I suspect, he tried to work out what was going on. 'Err... and that Ambrose chap. Any likely culprits?'

At this point the inspector took command. 'We rule no one in or out of our investigations, Colonel.'

Whipple's sudden change of tone, not to say miraculous recovery from his coughing fit, seemed to further confuse our host. 'I'm a suspect also?'

I thought the inspector's approach the act of a genius. 'To repeat, you are all suspects until proven otherwise to my satisfaction.'

Whipple's chilling assessment led the colonel to attempt humour by suggesting he might take the precaution of packing an overnight bag, since he'd heard such dreadful things about prison cells.

The inspector's stone-like expression did not alter, at which point HG ventured a comment about the garden. 'The flowers look divine at this time of the year, do they not, Crispen?'

HG's capacity to break the tension and guide events to her satisfaction never ceased to amaze me.

In contrast, the colonel merely looked around with disinterest. It was as if he'd only newly noticed nature's bounty, expertly manipulated by his employees.

'They are a testament to the skill and diligence the outdoor staff clearly have, and their loyalty to your family,' added HG.

The colonel looked bemused, waving a hand as if

swishing a wasp away. 'Yes, oh, yes, a fine bunch of men and women.

'Women?' responded Whipple.

I detected a note of triumph in the colonel's voice. 'Chief Inspector, it's 1922 after all. The butler informs me the housekeeper told him the head gardener told her we have employed a young lady to assist with dead-heading and suchlike.' The colonel lamented the paucity of staff because of factory workers and omnibus drivers being paid so much.

HG had clearly had enough of the colonel's domestic issues and brought matters to a head in her own inimitable way. 'Yes, yes, Crispen, all remarkably interesting I'm sure, but we must get a move on. As you said earlier, cocktails await.'

As we left the colonel wondering what had hit him, I reminded HG she didn't care for cocktails, to which I received a swift response. 'No, dear, but I saw Peregrine dashing up the stairs. We have our man.'

––––––––

'COCKTAILS WILL BE SERVED IN THE DRAWING ROOM IN FIFTEEN minutes, Your Grace.'

The butler's comment went unnoticed as HG led the way up the grand staircase at speed, leaving Whipple and me in her wake.

'And where might we find the colonel's son?' commanded the dowager as she continued her ascent.

'In his laboratory on the fourth floor,' came the distant response of a perplexed butler as the second floor beckoned us.

I observed the nature of the wall and ceiling decorations

and the materials used to construct the staircase becoming less ornate as we reached each floor.

Following a strange aroma to its source, we soon found ourselves outside a shabby door. HG came into her own once more by giving the flimsy door a single sharp tap before immediately opening it and promenading into the small, dingy room, which appeared squeezed under the eaves of the grand house.

I thought it curious that Peregrine simply continued with his work after offering a cursory glance in our direction. He pored over an experiment of some sort involving a lit Bunsen burner and ceramic dish, from which the foul odour detected outside appeared to emanate.

'May we have a word?' asked Whipple. Peregrine at first ignored the inspector's request. 'We could always do this at the police station. Might that be more convenient for you?'

The inspector's threat required no repetition. The colonel's son carefully put down the spatula he'd been using to agitate his noxious potion and stared blankly at Whipple.

'Tell me what you know of Ambrose Bagley.' The inspector's gruff manner left nothing to the imagination concerning his determination to elicit an answer.

'I know the man is dead. Unfortunate, but true.'

In a clever move, Whipple turned to HG and murmured about time wasted and that he'd need to continue the interview on police premises. His tone was loud enough for Peregrine to hear. It had the desired effect.

'To expand,' began the colonel's son, 'other than to say we shared an interest in botany. I therefore invited him down for the weekend so that we might share experiences and conduct several experiments.' Peregrine picked up the spatula again and began to stir the dish's contents.

HG interjected. 'A fellow botanist; how convenient. And how did you come to learn this?'

Peregrine went on at length to describe a symposium they attended some months previously and how they became colleagues through their shared passion.

By the time he'd finished his exposition on plants being categorised into two broad categories; non-vascular and vascular, and how certain examples fell into a particular genus, I felt the need to lie down in a darkened room.

I suspected Whipple thought the diatribe a distraction technique Peregrine employed to evade further pertinent questions about Ambrose. If this was the case, it did not fool Scotland Yard's finest. 'You meet a fellow once, months ago, then invite him to a shin-dig you probably did not know about until a few weeks ago? It makes no sense which, in my experience, tells me you're lying to an officer of His Majesty's police force. What have you to say to that?'

The assault accomplished his goal in prising open Peregrine's verbal armour. 'If you must know, Ambrose contacted me a few weeks ago to say he possessed several rare examples once owned by Darwin and retrieved from the Beagle itself. If true, it would've represented a significant discovery of items thought long lost.'

'And worth a pretty penny, I've no doubt? And an excellent motive for murder,' shot back the inspector.

Peregrine's response amazed me. Instead of panicking, the man smirked. 'I have no need of money. My father has more of the stuff than he knows what to do with.'

HG had the measure of the man and suggested that his interest lay in acquiring the specimens as a way of demonstrating his status as an eminent botanist to the professional establishment. 'Who knows,' said HG. 'Perhaps even an invitation to join The Royal Botanic Society?'

Whipple pressed home the argument. 'Did he renege on the deal? You had within your grasp the means to achieve the recognition you crave, only to have it snatched away by a man who took your money but failed to bring the specimens with him. Was he after more money? You argued. You killed him in a rage. That's what happened, isn't it?'

Inspector Whipple's deductions brought only a further snigger from his quarry. 'What silly games you play. Is this the best Scotland Yard offers?'

I was intrigued at first that Whipple chose not to retaliate, but say, 'I see. Then we shall leave you to press your buttercups or whatever they are.'

My education in the arts of interrogation took a further step forward as I realised his intention was to open Peregrine up like a can of beans.

'I have before me several prime examples of Atropa Belladonna if you must know.'

'Ah, deadly nightshade if I'm not mistaken, sir. A dangerous plant in the wrong hands, is it not?'

'Indeed it is inspector,' commented HG. 'Therefore, we should leave the gentleman to concentrate. Who knows what tragedy might befall a person who is careless with such a poison?'

The dowager turned to leave, encouraging Whipple and me to follow. As she reached for the door handle, she turned to face Peregrine. 'I almost forgot. You heard about the terrible accident in the lake last evening, did you not?'

The man's response was rapid and to the point. 'Morgan Prescott should have learned to swim.'

'Not a fan, then,' said HG. 'By the way, who told you his name?'

'I was in the drawing room last night, remember?'

'Oh, yes, I forgot. You didn't like that man either, did you?'

HG's marvellous parries to Peregrine's angst-driven responses provided a fine show of control over one's adversary.

'On another matter,' waded in the inspector. 'How well do you know Mr Norris?'

'The puppy, you mean. A spineless creature. If he were a botanical specimen, I wouldn't bother to press him, since there'd be little left under the slightest pressure.'

HG strolled a few feet back into the room to confront Peregrine. 'An odd thing to say, don't you think? You seem to find pleasure in the apparent weakness of others, isn't that so?'

'All I'm saying is he's always running after that silly Dosett girl. It makes me sick. If I were interested in her, I'd have rid myself of rivals and taken the woman for myself.'

'Did you?' said the dowager in a tone of deadly seriousness.

'Did I what?'

'Get rid of Ambrose Bagley because you have designs on her?'

8

SALMON AND POTATOES

Having foregone dinner with the other guests, I decided a visit to the local public house might yield useful information about the Percival-Travers family.

Although it had only just gone seven o'clock, the early evening atmosphere in the busy pub foreshadowed what I expected might be a raucous Saturday evening.

The Hope and Anchor looked like many across the land, with a date of 1776 cut into the lintel above the front door. Its location and large stable block pointed to the establishment's previous life as a coaching inn en route from Canterbury to London.

Inside the red brick building that sat beneath a thatched roof, the atmosphere was one of merriment and good-natured teasing between friends. As I'd expected, as soon as the locals caught sight of me entering, the place fell momentarily silent.

Stan Price, the colonel's gardener, hardly assisted matters by declaring, 'You again?'

I persevered and presented myself at Stan's oblong table, at which he sat playing dominos with three other men.

Intrigued at my appearance, one of them bade me take the weight off my feet and join them.

Observing four almost empty pewter tankards, I seized my opportunity to buy acceptance by offering to replenish, at my expense, the beer. At once I became one of them as if we were long-established friends. Only Stan continued to treat my presence with suspicion.

Beer replenished and domino game in full-swing, I broached the subject of Stan's employers to my new friends. Between bouts of intense concentration and shouts of 'knock-knock' when a player could not play his next move, useful titbits emerged.

When I asked if they thought the Percival-Travers a contented family, three of the men laughed, shoulders raising and lowering in time with one another. 'You don't want to believe what you see. Mr and Mrs can't stand one another. She's always going off on her own. Even her lady's maid don't know where her mistress goes.'

Foolishly, I asked how the man might know such a thing. My question led to hilarity among the group. 'Because my eldest is that maid.'

One of the other men chipped in. 'You know she's a spy, don't you? At least she was... in the war, I mean. She speaks perfect German. Don't know how, but she do.'

The third man observed, 'You know the war's been over for four years. I know you got a knock on the head at the Somme in '16, but even you must remember it's finished.'

Further hilarity followed as the friends chortled between themselves and swapped tales of daring-do in France. In his defence, the fellow said that just because the kaiser had abdicated, it didn't mean the Germans weren't up to their old tricks.

Stan soured the mood somewhat by declaring, 'What,

you mean like we do to them, like the French, and others. They're all as bad as one another and no good will come of it, you mark my words.'

Momentarily, Stan's friends looked sheepish, before breaking out into a further bout of riotous laughter and shouting over to the bar for another round of beer.

'Well, say what you will,' remarked the fellow who made the original accusation against the colonel's wife. 'But we've seen her meeting a man off the train. Rumour has it the colonel thinks his wife is having an affair, but what's to say they're not hiding messages in tree trunks and the like for the Germans. I watched a film the other week at the picture house and that's what them spies did – and they put secret messages in newspapers, you know, in the lost and found advertisements and suchlike.'

The reference reminded me of the scrap of newspaper I'd found by the lake's edge, which I resolved to look at again once I got indoors. As we continued to play dominos, at which I continued to suffer a thrashing, the rumour mill changed up a gear when I mentioned the two deaths on the estate. One man said his only surprise was that the victims were visitors and not staff.

When I asked what the man meant, he pointed his pipe at Stan.

'What you all looking at me for? That was a long time ago.'

Intrigued, I pushed for more information and after a few seconds of furtive glances between Stan Price's three companions, one spoke out.

'Some say they put the son, Peregrine, away when he was a lad. Around nine or ten. He almost killed a man who'd worked for his mother and father for years.'

I asked if the fellow still worked on the estate, to which Stan gave an astonishing answer.

'No, Peregrine cost my father his life.'

Slow to take in the awful news Stan delivered, I asked for clarification. 'Peregrine killed your father?'

Stan shrugged his shoulders and took a gulp from his pewter tankard. 'He rode a horse-drawn grass mower over my father's legs while dad tried to fix a linkage. Dad wouldn't have seen the boy take the reins. He didn't stand a chance. Crippled in both legs he was.'

I noted Stan's eyes burning with hatred as he spoke of Peregrine. At last, I realised where the source of the gardener's rage lay. Cautiously, I asked if the family looked after his father.

'They gave me his job, and his tied cottage. He lived with my Peggy and me until the end. Three years it took. I hate the lot of them.'

———

BY TEN O'CLOCK, THE TIME CAME FOR ME TO LEAVE THE HOPE and Anchor and head back to the servants' hall, my plan being to persuade Mable to find whatever food might be available since I'd missed servants' tea. As I completed the fifteen-minute walk from the pub to Bircham Manor, my mind raced with tales that ranged from spies to mechanical accidents, or murder, if Stan's view of events were true.

As I crossed the now familiar courtyard that led to the kitchen door, I entered with hesitation, unsure if my plan might work.

I need not have worried. My clandestine entrance met with Mable's smiling face. 'I wondered how long it would take for you to skulk in here. Sit down; I've kept something warmed up for you.'

Requiring no second invitation, I sat at the huge pine table and awaited Mable's delightful cooking. In seconds, a large plate of steaming-hot Irish stew sat before me. Brushing my copious thanks to one side, the delightful woman I enjoyed being around took the seat opposite as we gossiped about this and that, though not tales of spying or killing.

After several minutes, the tall, elegant figure of Doris Lovejoy, the cook, appeared at the door between the kitchen and main corridor leading to the service stairway. 'I thought I heard voices. What are you two up to then?' Mable and I smiled as Doris crossed the tiled floor with effortless grace and sat herself down next to her borrowed assistant. 'Is it good?' she said, pointing at the plate of stew. My smiled gave all the response she needed.

Doris proved easy to talk to, a characteristic rarely found among senior servants when a relative stranger invades their domain. Keen to validate what I'd learned from Stan and his drinking pals in the Hope and Anchor, I introduced the matter of the family's relationship with each other.

Unfortunately, the cook had worked on the estate for a little over five years, hence I had little to gain from talking about Stan Price's father. That said, Doris had her views on the Percival-Travers.

'All families go through their difficulties, don't they?' I agreed, urging Doris on.

'I have to say,' she continued, 'this family seems to have more downs than ups, if you'll forgive my lazy use of the English language.'

It seemed she, too, had observed a certain frostiness between the colonel and his wife after each of her sudden disappearances from the house, which sometimes, said Doris, lasted for over three days. Though Doris had heard them arguing about the matter, it seemed the colonel was less concerned with the absences than he was about being left with Peregrine.

I asked the cook if she might talk further on the topic. She revealed that most of the staff knew of Peregrine's habit of watching people. Visitors or staff, it appeared not to matter to the man. 'The colonel is aware of what his son gets up to and doesn't like it,' continued the cook. 'Yet he never chastises his son, which is something we lot don't understand.'

Until this point, Mable had remained silent. I assumed as a temporary member of staff, she was as interested in what went on in her adopted family as I. However, now, she contributed to the discussion. 'One housemaid told me the colonel's frightened of his son. He has a fearful temper, which his mother and father apparently call a blind fury.'

I looked to Doris for corroboration. 'Mable is correct. Mostly they keep it away from the staff, but when it's bad, you can hear them arguing wherever you're in the house.'

Before I could delve further, one of the service bells rang from a long line of such devices on a painted board with room names, which hung on the wall behind Mable and Doris. The cook swivelled around to check which room called. 'It's Dr Griffiths. He didn't come down for dinner, so he'll be wanting some supper. It's ready for him. Will one of you take it up or should I call for a footman?'

Seizing an opportunity to ask the good doctor several questions, I readily volunteered. Having climbed the many stairs required to reach the third floor, I sympathised with staff having to make the journey many times a day.

Giving the fine oak-panelled door a sharp tap, I entered

to see the doctor's welcoming grin as he caught sight of his supper. 'Come in, do come in. Set it down there, will you? Thank you so much.'

Expecting me to leave the room, the doctor offered a further smile, which turned to mild confusion as I remained standing at the small table upon which I had laid his supper.

'Can I help?' he said, to which I replied the dowager had tasked me with asking one or two questions about the recent tragedies at the great house. I knew that HG would have no objection to such subterfuge. On the contrary, she'd expect me to engage such tactics.

At first sullen at the interruption, Dr Griffiths soon rallied as I lifted a silver domed cover to reveal a plate of Scottish pink salmon and small boiled potatoes, garnished with baby tomatoes and basil.

Taking the precaution of allowing the doctor to take several bites of his supper, I gently introduced the topic of death, which, looking back, appeared a contradiction in terms. However, Dr Griffiths obliged my clumsy attempt to gather information.

'How will we know if Morgan Prescott drowned, you say? Quite simple. During the post-mortem, we shall look for water in the poor fellow's lungs. If none is present, then he was already dead when he hit the water. Should water be present, the reverse will be the case and, despite any injury he suffered by whatever means, the man simply drowned.'

The starkness of the doctor's fact-based approach brought home to me what a dreadful end Mr Prescott suffered. 'If the former, then it implies murder, does it not?' I asked.

Dr Griffiths shrugged his shoulders as he took aim at a boiled potato with a silver fork.

'And Ambrose Bagley?'

Finishing a glass of port I'd poured the doctor from a lead-crystal decanter, he wiped the remnants from his lips with a brilliant white napkin and held an index finger up. 'There is no doubt the man received a blow to the skull, yet the injury appears relatively benign. You might expect the man to suffer a headache, even concussion, but death? I'm puzzled about that one. Again, we shall know more after the post-mortem.'

———

As I EXITED THE DOCTOR'S ROOM HOLDING HIS SUPPER TRAY, my mind wandered as I pondered the implications of what he'd told me, when a voice called out.

'I see you're being put to good use.' The teasing tone belonged to the dowager and our paths met in the spacious hallway of the splendid house. 'Come and join Whipple and me in the library, though you may wish to deposit that tray in the kitchen first to avoid permanent employment as a footman.' HG continued to grin as she swept through the hallway and disappeared.

'Sherry?' asked the inspector as I settled into a luxurious leather Chesterfield in the comfy library. Having declined his offer, I immediately updated my two companions on my discussion with Dr Griffiths, as well as what I'd gleaned from Stan and his pals, plus Mable and Doris in the servants' quarters.

Whipple acknowledged he was becoming nervous regarding the time remaining to catch one, or possibly two, killers. 'I don't have the authority to keep these people here. They will disperse after breakfast on Monday and there is little I can do.'

I suggested he might arrest one or two on suspicion of murder, to which he replied there was a minor matter of evidence. 'And once I let someone go for lack of evidence, it's much harder to re-arrest them, especially this lot.'

HG grinned as she placed her sherry glass onto the lustrous surface of a French-polished table-top. 'He means toffs like me.'

I watched the inspector as his cheeks coloured, which amused HG even more.

'Oh, Arthur, all these years of working together and I can still make you blush. I shall take that as a compliment.'

The dowager's comment made Whipple even more self-conscious as he clumsily took a gulp from the tiny sherry glass.

'Now, to business. How shall we resolve matters?'

HG's forthright comment had the effect of helping Whipple gather his senses, or perhaps the dowager knew this might assist her friend in overcoming his temporary embarrassment.

Suddenly revived, the inspector felt for his Everton mints and, after offering them around, popped one into his mouth. 'There are two matters requiring attention as a matter of urgency.' Putting an open hand to his right cheek as if checking the mint hadn't broken a tooth, the inspector continued. 'First, we must pay a further visit to the lakeside to see if any blood is present. If there is, it will prove Morgan Prescott received his injury on land. It won't determine whether he died there, or by what means, but it's a start.

'And the second action?' asked HG.

'We must interview Augustine's lady's maid to see what she can tell us about her mistress.'

I suggested the lady's maid was likely to be most loyal to her employer, which HG dismissed in a heartbeat.

'Don't you believe it. A lady's maid will attempt to convince her mistress she is oblivious to the most intimate conversations she will overhear, while all the while collecting them for gossip. However, an intelligent mistress will know this and play the lady's maid like a fiddle, acting as a purveyor of planted information. If Augustine Percival-Travers is anything, she's intelligent.'

9

A PERKY PIKE

R elieved the vicar limited his Sunday morning sermon to twenty minutes, I joined the houseguests in a pleasant stroll back from St Martins to the Bircham Manor via a delightful water meadow in the last throws of its summer show of wildflowers.

For once, all appeared peaceful, with even the Watkins-Simms brothers getting on. As I looked over the soft land-scape across to the village, with its mix of thatched and tiled roofs attached to ancient buildings, HG sidled up to me.

'I have no desire to partake in the horse trail the colonel has arranged for everyone. Instead, I wish to speak to Augustine's lady's maid to see what she might know. Can you find her and tell her there is a delicate matter on which I wish to consult, and I shall be in the summer house?'

My instructions clear, I set off in pursuit of the maid. This turned out to be no simple task, since the woman hadn't attended church, meaning she wasn't among the group of staff that dawdled someway behind their employers and weekend guests.

Eventually, I found the woman passing the time of day

with a footman, whose company she appeared to enjoy. Following a few seconds of confusion when she assumed it was the footman I wished to speak to, I prised her away from her companion.

Explaining the matter was a delicate one, I invited the maid to join the dowager as soon as might be convenient, which I pressed upon the woman meant presently. Clearly pleased at being summoned by a duchess, she took little persuading.

Having introduced each to one another, I stepped from the summerhouse and closed a pair of glass-panelled doors behind me. Fortunately, because of several windows being open, I could still hear their conversation.

I was impressed at the tale HG spun about having borrowed an item of clothing from the maid's mistress some weeks previous, a lace cuff of which she had unfortunately damaged, and the dowager wished to know if the lady's maid might fix the item before having to inform her good friend.

Having drawn the woman into her web, HG cleverly steered the conversation around to the movements of Augustine, vis-a-vis her meeting a stranger off the train. At first, the maid denied all knowledge of such behaviour. However, the dowager's hint that a senior position was soon to be available within her household on superior terms to those she currently enjoyed loosened the maid's tongue.

Augustine's maid went further in divulging information than I expected, a position HG was sure to have concurred with. Each time her employer visited London, it was always to the same Knightsbridge address, she told us. It turned out the maid knew this for certain since a cousin was the butler in a house opposite the one visited by the colonel's wife.

When HG asked her about matters more local, the maid

appeared to know immediately to what the dowager referred. Augustine often met a man dressed in a pinstriped suit, who always brought flowers. They never came back to the house and would, instead, disappear into thin air for one hour, after which she'd wave the gentleman off on his London-bound journey.

What she couldn't tell HG was whether the person her mistress visited in London was the same person she met off the train. I found this new intelligence fascinating and waited with bated breath to discuss the matter with HG.

The dowager then asked a question I found to be curious. She wished to know what type of flowers the man gave Augustine, assuming she brought them back with her.

'Oh, yes,' replied the maid. 'She gets me to put them in a vase in her bedroom. Heaven knows what the master must think when he comes through from his own bedroom.'

'And the species of flowers?' HG persisted, to which the maid said that they were orchids or carnations, which, she said, meant that the gentleman must have glass houses, given the time of year the flowers sometimes appeared. She concluded by saying, 'So I wonder which it shall be this afternoon.'

The dowager was on this remark like a kestrel hovering above a field mouse.

'Oh, yes,' the maid said when questioned by HG. 'The 2.30 pm from London.'

———

AFTER COMPARING NOTES ONCE AUGUSTINE'S MAID HAD LEFT the summerhouse, HG noted she had one or two things to check out, and that I should seek the inspector.

'Church interesting?' he enquired before adding, 'I don't hold with such things.'

Determining his words more of a statement than a question, I concentrated instead on the conditions of his hands, which were grubby. Announcing he'd carried out a thorough fingertip search, Whipple plunged a dirty hand into his suit pocket and retrieved a brown paper bag.

Quite looking forward to another Everton toffee boiled sweet, I found my disappointment hard to conceal when he offered me sight of the bag's contents.

'I'll wager this gold chain is from the missing pocket watch belonging to Mr Ambrose Bagley.'

Immediately realising the significance of the find, I felt somewhat guilty at coveting confectionary over evidence.

'I shall have a word with my constables about this. They should have found this on Friday,' said Whipple, to which I gave silent thanks not to be one of those young officers.

I asked Whipple why he thought the chain must belong to Ambrose. Without touching the glistening ribbon of precious metal, he pointed to its clean appearance. 'Of course, gold does not tarnish or degrade like all other metals, but there isn't a sign of dirt or any other detritus on this chain. It is, therefore, my view that it has only recently found itself deposited among the woodland floor.'

Taking a further look into the paper bag, I pondered how the accessory came to rest in such a position and asked the inspector as much.

Whipple determined the chain dislodged itself from the watch shortly after the timepiece fell or was stolen from Ambrose's waistcoat. 'Perhaps his assailant, in a panic to flee the scene, failed to notice the chain falling to the floor.'

It occurred to me that if this was the case, the man

concerned might return to the murder scene to retrieve damning evidence of his guilt.

The inspector thought this a plausible deduction. He noted that although likely the murderer may already have attempted to find it, there might be a case for staking the area out when darkness fell to lie in wait. 'Such activities are usually a waste of time. However, we have the constables to do it, so we may get lucky.'

Whipple took me to the location in which he found the chain and instructed me on what sort of thing a thorough detective takes into consideration when searching for evidence. 'Foremost,' he began, 'it is of the utmost importance not to unduly disturb the crime scene or, in this case, the search area. Notice how clean the area is. No one might know I'd been here if I say so myself.'

I pointed to several small broken overhanging branches as evidence he'd not been quite as nymph-like as he thought. As I expected, the inspector did not take my comments well. At least, not until he grasped the significance of my discovery.

'Do you notice anything about those branches?'

I realised immediately that this amounted to Whipple's attempt to regain credibility, though I considered this never to be in doubt. I shrugged my shoulder and the inspector smiled.

'Do you notice they're all broken in the same direction?' He held his arm above his head and mimicked a slashing action, as if breaking through the undergrowth in an Amazonian forest.

On closer inspection, I realised the inspector held a valid position. 'What might have caused such damage?' I asked.

Whipple appeared deep in thought for a few seconds,

before a self-satisfied smile spread across his work-aged features. 'A tennis racket.'

———

RATHER THAN TAKE THE ROLLS, THE DOWAGER DECLARED WE'D walk to the station, that way, she declared, we might keep our arrival incognito.

Certainly, the walk from Bircham Manor into the hamlet was a most pleasant affair as we sauntered along a country lane devoid of passing company, other than a curious horse, which popped its head over a trimmed hawthorn hedge, perhaps to enquire if a carrot might be on offer.

As we rounded a gentle corner of the narrow lane having left Whipple working on the case, we caught our first sight of Whiston Magna. HG commented that if this was the larger of the two settlements that made up this tiny corner of Kent, she couldn't guess at the population of Whiston Parva.

Hearing the village clock situated high on the Norman bell tower of the church, I noted we had a full fifteen minutes to cover the remaining short distance from our current location to the train station. All appeared under control until we passed the village farrier and were greeted by a fellow in a brown leather apron and flat cap one might see worn in the industrial north of England.

I recognised the man immediately as one of Stan's drinking partners from the Hope and Anchor. A genial fellow with a ready smile. Having removed his cap to greet the dowager, whom he had not seen before, the chap then turned his attention to me and offered a friendly greeting.

Unaware of our urgent mission, the man chatted away as if he'd all day to dawdle, which, judging by the contented looking Clydesdale horse being shoed, he may well have had.

Attempting to extricate ourselves from the situation for fear of missing the train's arrival, we almost bid the fellow farewell when he enquired if the police had detained the Beast of Bircham Manor. I thought it astounding that a local populous was so readily persuaded by gossip that contorted rumours might so readily morph into local folklore.

HG oozed charm as she assured the farrier of all our best efforts and thanked the chap for his enquiry. About to leave, having taken a further anxious look at the church clock that now read four minutes until two thirty, our escape stuttered to a halt when the farrier made a startling statement.

It seemed a local observed a drunken man on the colonel's estate on Friday. Specifically, by the edge of the lake, and the villager reckoned him to be the murderer of Ambrose Bagley, whom the farrier identified as 'that fella'.

If true, the farrier's astounding revelation amounted to an eyewitness account of, if not a murder, then it's immediate aftermath.

Interest sparked, the dowager thanked the man for his news and commented on how observant the villagers had been. She pondered if the farrier knew the identity of said gentleman.

When called for, HG deployed a guile capable of rendering her quarry unable to resist her will. And so it was with the farrier. Although at first reluctant to say more, he quickly changed his tune when HG produced five shillings from a silver chain purse she always carried about her person.

'Three-fingers Freddie,' said the farrier, holding his right hand up with the index and middle fingers clasped against his palm to reinforce the description.

A further question from HG on where she might find such a fellow met with further resistance until a third half-a-crown emerged from the dowager's purse.

'He's a poacher who lives here and there. He's always on the colonel's estate,' declared the farrier. 'Reckons there's good pickings from the lake and woodland.'

Unable to contain my curiosity, I asked about his reference to the poacher's fingers.

'Lost two of them tickling for trout on the lake. Three-fingers is always telling us he's an expert at tickling fish to catch them. Of course, that was before he had his run-in with Razor-Gob.'

'Razor err...' sputtered the dowager.

'Razor-Gob. He's the old pike. The beast was there when I was a teenager, so heaven knows how old it is, but he's huge with a set of gnashers to go with it and he doesn't take prisoners. Now poor old Three-fingers has real trouble picking his nose, I can tell you.'

Thankfully, the sound of a train whistle excluded further exploration of the poacher's personal habits and forced HG and me to offer hasty thanks and take our leave of the surprised farrier.

Covering the final hundred yards to the station at an unseemly speed, especially for a lady wearing a long narrow dress and dainty hat, we arrived in time to observe the train pulling into the station, its green livery glistening in the afternoon sun. As we passed a station sign that read Whiston Halt, the familiarity of the name struck a chord that I could not immediately place as HG hurried me to follow.

Safely ensconced behind a porter's flat trolly piled high

with suitcases and other assorted luggage, we quicky identified Augustine as she waited for the train to come to a stop
as steam and coal smoke poured from its impressive engine.

The colonel's wife continued her patient vigil until a
gaggle of passengers disembarked, some lingering to greet
friends and relatives. Eventually, a tall, elegant man dressed
in an impeccable pinstriped suit emerged from a cloud of
steam, holding a small bunch of flowers.

We watched as the fellow closed the distance between
himself and the colonel's wife, his smile broadening as they
met. She held her right, gloved hand in front of her, and the
man took hold and gently laid a kiss on the white fabric,
before handing over the flowers.

It was then I felt a sharp tug on my arm. 'We must leave
immediately. That man must not see me. Come away, now.'

10

THE LADY FAINTS

The dowager acted out of character as we made our way back to Bircham Manor. It seemed the man she'd seen meeting Augustine had ruffled her normally smooth feathers. When I asked who the fellow was, she at first refused to discuss the matter.

Unwilling to accept the situation, I persevered as we left the environs of Whiston Magna and headed out into open country for the few minutes before we sighted our host's wonderful home.

'Let us simply say knowing that chap's position in life places Augustine in an interesting position, which I shall divulge to you when appropriate.'

I'd known HG long enough not to pursue the matter further and settled for a genial conversation about the pleasant August weather, before encountering the Clydesdale once again.

'Do you think he's moved an inch since we saw him last?' said HG, whereupon we agreed to name the magnificent beast Arthur, in honour of Inspector Whipple. This was decided on the basis that neither appeared to hurry, though one would not wish to get on the wrong side of either.

Keen to update the said inspector, even if HG did not intend to divulge all she knew, we set out about tracking him down. Absent from his usual haunt of the buffet table and failing to occupy his hideaway, the library, we resorted to taking a turnabout of the grounds.

Everyone we came across said they had not seen the inspector. Just as we turned back to the great house, a strange sound, a sort of grunting noise, filled the air.

Expecting to find a distressed animal of some sort, we followed the tuneless din into a dense thicket, persevering because of the urgency of the call until we reached a tiny clearing. Here we found the chief inspector swinging a tennis racket and dodging from side to side as if fighting for match point at Wimbledon.

Since Whipple had his back to us, the inspector didn't know he had an audience willing him on. After several seconds of enjoying the spectacle of a middle-aged detective in work suit and hat, ducking and diving at an unseen opponent, HG offered a lady-like cough. Her first attempt failed to garner his attention. The dowager's second attempt sounded more like someone requiring an elixir for pneumonia.

Not only did the gruff clearing of her throat startle me, but it also caused Whipple to lose concentration and trip forward. Only the nimblest of moves and the fortunate intervention of a nearby hedge stopped the fellow from belly flopping onto the compacted earth.

Clearing his own throat and getting to his feet as if his display of acrobatics were the most natural thing in the world, Whipple insisted we had happened upon him undertaking vital police research.

'Of course, dear Arthur,' said the dowager, picking a selection of dried leaves and twigs from his person.

I restricted myself to offering the man a compliment on the dexterity of his backhand and asked if he might show me how to do it.

Enjoying the recognition of his prowess as a competent player, the inspector bade me step forward, handed over his racket and instructed me on the finer points of the game, insisting it was all about balance, without the slightest sense of irony as he rubbed his right kneecap.

Watching proceedings with a peculiar expression reminiscent of an indulgent mother pondering the foolishness of her children, HG held a finger up, which we knew to be an instruction to pay attention.

'How wide did Dr Griffiths declare the weapon that inflicted Ambrose's head wound must be?' she asked.

Closing my eyes and taking a second to recall the dreadful scene to my conscious mind, I had the answer. 'I should say a little under one inch,' I replied.

Stepping forward to relieve me of my sports equipment, HG surveyed the racket edge-on. 'Which approximates the thickness of this, does it not?'

Whipple and I exchanged a look of astonishment at the dowager's powers of observation and skills in making a deduction there from.

The inspector gestured for the racket, which HG obligingly handed over. 'This could do some damage,' he said before lifting the wooden implement strung with gut above his head and bringing it crashing down, edge-on.

'But could it kill?' asked the dowager.

Whipple inspected the edge of the racket and felt its uneven surface caused by the stringing. 'I suppose it's possible. However, a substantial amount of force is required to inflict anything other than a superficial cut, or one requiring a few stitches at most if you were unlucky.'

'But you don't rule out the possibility that such a thing might kill?'

The inspector raised his eyebrows at HG before commenting that she sounded too much like the prosecuting council in a murder trial, clutching at straws to gain a guilty verdict on some hapless soul. 'There is one sure way to find out. If a tennis racket was used to kill Ambrose Bagley, then the injury should show signs of the stringing pattern.' Whipple once again ran a finger along the edge of his racket.

'Then to Dr Griffiths. Let us determine if he's had the results of Ambrose's post-mortem.'

———

FRUSTRATED AT DR GRIFFITHS' ABSENCE, HG SUGGESTED WE take a turn around the lake by boat, if only to escape the trail ride the colonel had arranged. 'I cannot abide riding horses,' commented HG. 'It seems to me, clambering over an animal that might reasonably be expected to begrudge, then being at the thing's mercy to keep you alive, is an object lesson in lunacy.'

I shared the dowager's aversion to horsepower unless it lived under the bonnet of a motor vehicle. The inspector fell unusually quiet and at first, I thought it because of his exertion with the tennis racket. Not so. Whipple eventually revealed all.

'I have a natural dislike of water that doesn't come out of a tap.'

HG offered him a stark choice: horse riding or thirty minutes in a perfectly sound watercraft. Rather churlishly he selected the latter and followed HG and me to the water's edge. His bearing was that of a child calling on his least favourite relative for afternoon tea, where even the lure of lemonade and current cake could not overcome his fear of having to sit still for an hour.

As we reached the beached boat, the sound of blowing and snorting horses, unhappy with their lot, floated in the still air.

'I suggest you made the correct decision, Arthur,' said HG as a scream, followed by a thump of someone hitting the ground hard, reinforced the dowager's position.

Having pushed the small craft into the water, I held it steady so that HG could clamber aboard, then the inspector followed. From the second he nervously sat on the hard wooden plank that served as his seat, he grabbed each side of the craft with white-knuckled hands and refused to let go.

After positioning two long timber oars in their respective rowlocks, I heaved hard and propelled us from the shore and onward to the centre of the still waters of the colonel's lake.

HG came to life as she directed me to row one way, then another, clearly at home on the water. The ocean blue it may not have been. However, in the dowager's minds-eye, I suspected, we were pirates upon the high seas, or Nelson about to have a mixed day at Trafalgar.

'Isn't it a wonderful sight?' said the dowager as she stretched her arms wide to emphasise the beauty of the countryside found in Kent. 'What more could one ask for, apart from a picnic, that is.'

Even Whipple relaxed as we cruised along the shimmering surface of the lake. An artificial construct it may have been, but no less breath-taking for that. I suggested that Capability Brown, who had designed and built the garden, had much to congratulate himself on.

To my astonishment, the inspector even let go of the boat. I suspected this caused him some pain as the blood rushed back into his fingers. But allowing his numb digits to dangle into the clear, cool, waters seemed to please the fellow no end.

At the same time, I sensed, as I observed his eyes darting from one part of the boat to the next, that as a true detective, he never fully relaxed. At first, I assumed his recent water-based anxiety had returned. However, I was mistaken.

'If Morgan Prescott was bundled out of this boat by person – or persons – unknown, they were professionals. Look around you. Not a sign of them or a struggle to lift a body over the side, never mind if the man was still alive and fighting for his life.'

HG started then jettisoned her reply when the inspector jumped from his seat, before realising where he was and quickly sitting down again. 'What the...' was all he said before looking at the water with eyes as big as gobstoppers.

'What's wrong, man?' summed up HG's response as she bade the inspector sit still or we'd all end up in the lake.

'There's a shark in that water,' exclaimed the agitated inspector as he pointed at the still waters. HG's assertion such a suggestion boarded on the preposterous did nothing to move Whipple regarding the justice of his position, as he held two cut fingertips up as evidence. 'Alright,' he said, 'you put your hand in and see what happens.' The challenge was a general one and not aimed at the dowager specifically.

Unperturbed, but hedging her bets, HG picked up the end of our mooring rope and dangled it over the edge before allowing its tip to slip beneath the water's surface. In an instant, we detected a thrashing movement and splashing of water as something took hold of the rope. As HG pulled on the rope, the mighty set of backwards-facing teeth of a huge pike came into view.

'It's Razor-Gob,' I offered.

Whipple looked at me as if I'd lost all sense, compounded by HG's statement. 'Then the farrier was telling the truth. Find that poacher we must.'

———

RETURNING TO SHORE HAVING FINALLY PERSUADED THE ILL-tempered pike to allow us our mooring rope back, we beached the craft as the inspector wrapped a handkerchief around the two fingers Razor-Gob got its teeth into.

'There's that gardener fellow. What's his name? Oh, yes, Stan Price,' commented HG as we wandered by the house, having mulled over whether Morgan Prescott met his end at the hands of one or more men.

'Price is strange,' I replied and reminded my companions that he'd made a barbed comment to the boot boy about 'hating them all'.

HG picked up on my comment by pondering if the gardener meant the Percival-Travers or the leisured class per se. 'If the latter,' she added, 'what better way to get some sort of revenge than by killing two of them in a secluded spot by the lake-edge?'

I dissented by pointing out the time that had passed since his father received his injury and died years later.

Whipple had his own take on the situation. 'I've seen such things before. Hate builds up over the years, then suddenly it erupts into senseless violence for no apparent reason. It's as if by hurting others, the individual gains relief and releases his feelings.'

Before we could explore the matter further, a distressed young woman ran toward us from the house. Rowena Dosett collapsed into Inspector Whipple's arms. 'Please, help me, Inspector. A man... bedroom... hurt me.'

HG immediately produced smelling salts, which she once told me to be a boon for all unusual occurrences. Within seconds, Rowena coughed as the noxious mixture did its foul-smelling work. Some minutes passed before Miss Dosett felt able to explain what had brought her to such a sad situation.

'I was taking a nap before afternoon tea when I detected a strange noise. Opening my eyes, I saw a shadow. The curtains were closed. It was hard to see. Then I felt...' Rowena almost lost consciousness again, stopped only by the dowager's second application of smelling salts. 'I felt a pain. My head.' Miss Dosett lifted a hand to her left temple and dabbed it with a dainty lace kerchief. 'Why should anyone wish to hurt me?'

This time, Rowena's faint was complete.

'Let the girl be for a few minutes,' said HG as Miss Dosett reposed on the trimmed lawn of Bircham Manor.

11

TWO BOWLER HATS

With Miss Dosett put to bed in another bedroom under the supervision of the dowager and a maid, the inspector and I surveyed the crime scene.

Chief among our considerations was why anyone, let alone a houseguest, might wish to harm the lady. All appeared normal as far as one could tell, with no disturbance to the room's furnishings, fittings or contents belonging to Rowena.

'We know Lemuel Norris is smitten by the lady,' began the inspector. 'Perhaps so is Peregrine Percival-Travers, though for what reason I don't yet know. One likely scenario is that one or the other attacked in a fit of romantic jealousy. You know, being spurned. That kind of thing.'

My logic followed much of what Whipple expounded, though I, too, found it hard to equate Peregrine with romance. Still, it's said that opposites often attract, yet from the evidence presented and observation of the strange fellow since our arrival on Friday, it seemed implausible to suspect our wayward botanist on those grounds.

As we continued our search for anything that might lead

us to Miss Dosett's attacker, the dowager joined us. 'She's resting now. Hopefully, a decent sleep will help restore her constitution from that terrible act of barbarity.'

I applauded HG's sentiments and redoubled my efforts to discover something of use to our investigations. 'But were not all the guests out riding with the colonel and his family? Given we were on the lake, that only leaves whichever servants remained, or an intruder?' Pleased with my assessment of the situation, I awaited congratulations from the inspector.

Alas, the fellow took a different view. 'But how do we know who did or did not go riding; which members of staff remained, or if a stranger is among us?'

HG agreed with the inspector and reminded us that time was short before all were to leave the our wonderful lodgings after breakfast on Monday. 'Therefore,' she announced, 'my view is that we should prioritise our efforts by confirming the whereabouts of Messrs Lemuel and Percival at the time the attack took place. After that, we shall see what we shall see.'

As HG spoke, the inspector continued with his diligent visual sweep of the room. He moved the bed, then gently pulled back the light cotton sheets and silk bedspread that had covered its occupant. 'Look here,' he said, leaning forward to inspect an Egyptian cotton pillow. 'Blood.'

His startling revelation led the dowager and me to join the inspector. Now three heads occupied a position side by side, a few inches from evidence of violence.

'What might have caused such a result?' asked HG as the inspector scoured the immediate area for additional signs of disturbance.

'They attacked Miss Dosett while she lay in bed, that's for sure. In my estimation the cause of her injury was a blunt object, otherwise, we should have found more copious amounts of blood. Two questions arise: what and why?'

Whipple bade us undertake a fingertip search of the room while he concentrated on the bed. After a few minutes, Whipple muttered, frustrated that no further evidence was available from the Tudor four-poster bed.

HG came to our rescue by pointing to a silver-gilt cigarette case on the floor, almost out of sight, under a bedroom cupboard on the same side as the bed where Whipple discovered the blood.

'He must have knocked it off the table in his rush to escape, or, of course, dropped it after seizing the thing from the table and hitting his victim with it. Miss Dosett told us she awoke to see a shadow. We must assume the man panicked.'

I enquired how the inspector knew the cigarette case already occupied its position on the table when the attacker entered, instead of belonging to the beastly creature himself.

Whipple pointed to the top surface of the bedside table. 'Striking matches in an identically designed silver-gilt case.'

I felt tempted to kick myself for missing such an obvious clue. A sympathetic smile from HG told me she, too, had made the connection.

Crouching down, HG carefully retrieved the ornate cigarette case, taking care not to touch it directly, instead utilising a lace kerchief she always kept tucked inside a sleeve of her gown. Carefully laying the object on the bed, giving first one face then the other close scrutiny, she shook her head. 'What isn't here, Rex?'

The dowager's question put me on the spot. My mind raced as I looked upon the gleaming silver.

As I took a few seconds too long to respond, the

inspector answered HG's question for me. 'Blood. The victim's blood is absent. Had this been the weapon used to inflict her injury, then evidence of it striking its victim would remain.'

I continued to remain confused as to why such an attack should occur now, though the thought of someone watching Miss Dosett's every move to plan his attack chilled me to the bone.

My meanderings came to a halt as the maid charged with looking after Miss Dosett entered the room to report the victim sound asleep, courtesy of the doctor's administration of laudanum.

'Then I'll post one of my constables directly outside Miss Dosett's room to discourage further disturbance, or any attempt by the depraved soul who carried out the attack to complete his dreadful work.'

HG graciously dismissed the maid by thanking her for the close attention paid to Miss Dosett and made clear her intention to inform the colonel to that effect.

All that remained now was to evacuate the room and lock the door to bar further entry until the inspector gave orders to the contrary.

'Now,' said the dowager as we stood in the wide corridor outside the bedroom. 'I think afternoon tea in the orangery is called for. Follow me, men.'

———

ALTHOUGH OUR PARTY ARRIVED FIRST, WHICH WHIPPLE TOOK full advantage of by filling his plate, the other houseguests soon entered. I noticed one or two nursing various bruises and scratches to the face and assumed some were clearly more competent on horseback than others.

As I continued to gaze upon a gaggle of tired faces and aching backs, HG drew our attention to who was not present. 'Neither Lemuel nor Peregrine are here. Do we regard this as unusual, given our earlier conversation in Rowena's bedroom?'

Unable to contain her curiosity, before either the inspector or I could respond, the dowager made off for the colonel. We followed as if a pair of sausage dogs expecting a treat from their master.

'My son detests the hobby for some strange reason. As for the other fellow, Lemuel, you say. Well, it seems he had an errand to run. If you ask me, it sounded a little fishy.'

HG suggested perhaps Percival had suffered a traumatic event with a horse when a child. She added such things can often linger into adulthood.

'Trauma, child?' replied the colonel as he spat out more of the cucumber sandwich than he'd eaten. 'Augustine's child was as bonkers then as he is now. From what I remember, the fellow showed little interest in horses or fishing, bally difficult as that is to believe. All he wanted to do was look at flowers... and watch people. Still does it, you know.' The colonel shook his head and bit into a cream fancy and cucumber sandwich concurrently, seeming not to notice the unusual combination of ingredients.

HG swooped on the reference to his son as 'Augustine's child', suggesting it a peculiar description to use about his own flesh and blood.

Dispatching the last of his fancy into his mouth with the tip of a forefinger, the colonel shrugged his shoulders. 'I served overseas sporadically between 1880 and 1901. Augustine mostly remained in England. Who knows, these things happen. Anyway, he serves his purpose as my heir.'

'But no spare,' said HG light-heartedly.

The colonel thought for a few seconds before seeing off a second cream fancy. 'Oh... yes, I see. Exceedingly funny. No, no spare. I spent a great deal of time at my club, rather than... well. Ah, there's Witchingham. I went to school with him, you know. Must catch up on old times...'

Resisting the temptation to erupt into a trio of giggles, we averted our eyes from our fleeing host and, instead, each concentrated on our own plates of deliciousness.

Seeing our levity, the wives of the Watkins-Simms twins meandered over to our position. Of course, respect for our host prevented any disclosure concerning Peregrine's parental origins.

Instead, HG commented their husbands appeared to be getting on well, judging by their illuminated features as they sat chatting in a corner of the large orangery like a pair of naughty school children.

The elder's wife commented we had observed them at their worst the previous day, yet today they would kill for each other. The lady checked herself as she observed Whipple's eyes narrowing. 'Oh, forgive me,' she said as her cheeks flushed. 'My flippant remark is unconscionable given the current circumstances. But they have always been the same. We leave them to it unless things go too far.'

The younger's wife supported her sister-in-law. 'Of course, it might have been worse; it isn't unknown for them to set about one another with their tennis rackets. Their parents say they were as bad at school. Because they're identical twins, they were apparently always claiming elder was younger, or the other way around, to avoid the headmaster's array of punishments. Be in no doubt, one will always cover for the other, whatever the reason.'

As we three digested the wives' fascinating and potentially useful insight into their spouses, Augustine breezed over, seemingly as absent minded as ever, to ask if everyone enjoyed the fishing.

'Horse riding, Augustine. Everyone went riding,' said HG with a certain edge to her words. 'And what have you been up to, my dear?'

Augustine replied it had been such a boring day, present company excepted, while lamenting how much effort it took to run Bircham Manor. 'Do you know, Eleanor, I haven't seen so much as a ray of sunshine today, so occupied have I been with matters concerning staff discipline. Most distasteful.'

I could tell from the dowager's general demeanour that the game was afoot. 'How strange, Augustine, because I looked everywhere for you.'

HG's assessment of our host as a consummate actor shone forth. 'Really? What was it you wanted?' Augustine wrung a portion of her shoulder-length auburn hair around a finger as if attempting a curl, while looking unseeingly into the distance.

'Oh, nothing of importance. I wondered if the post had gone since I had an urgent communication to send. In the end, Rex and I took a stroll into the village to locate a post-box.'

I noted Augustine moved not a muscle, save for her eyes, which blinked at an unusually fast rate. 'Post... Oh, did you, dear? I find the postal service a little lacking these days. What say you?' HG failed to respond, leaving Augustine to blink more furiously. 'Ah, I see I'm required by one of my staff. There is such a great deal of work to do to maintain standards these days.'

In a second, our host took her leave. In fact, Augustine left the room without speaking to either guest or staff member.

'It seems Augustine can see through walls, since clearly, no member of staff required her attention here.'

HG's comment left me in no doubt that she had Augustine in her sights.

———

As we wandered into the large hallway, Inspector Whipple, content that afternoon tea met his gastronomic needs, looked in good spirits. That was until we saw the butler remonstrating with two burly fellows in workaday black suits and bowler hats.

'Can a policeman not have five minutes to himself without having to quell a threat to the King's peace?'

I had some sympathy for his position after the busy day we'd had. HG marched to the door and ordered the two men to be silent. People did what the dowager required when she spoke in that certain way and adopted the imperious stance one might find in a formal portrait of the monarch.

'Are you two tradespersons of some description? If so, why are you at the front door of this noble house?'

The dowager's act amused Whipple and me no end, since we both knew her impressive display of pomposity was about as far from her actual personality as it was possible to get.

Her intervention even raised the hint of a smile from the butler's usually more surly demeanour. To reinforce support for the fellow, Whipple marched to the front entrance and demanded to know why the two strangers had upset Lomas.

The butler said he'd found the men lurking outside and enquired what business they were about. Having not been furnished with anything that made sense, he told them to leave, to which they objected.

'I tried to explain certain matters about–

HG cut him off. 'No need to explain, Lomas. Please show these gentlemen into the library, where we shall join them shortly.'

Making no attempt to hide his confusion, the butler did as HG instructed, leaving Whipple and me to gather our thoughts.

'Follow my lead when we get in there,' said the dowager, which, I suspected, meant she'd already formulated her plan.

Entering the library with a flourish, the dowager strode over to the men, who stood one each side of the great fireplace, bowler hats in hand and not quite knowing where to look.

'I am Eleanor, Dowager Duchess of Drakeford.'

One man nodded his head as a mark of respect, the other, shorter and stouter than his colleague, half-bowed and half-curtsied, which HG made no comment upon.

'And you are?' she said, her imperious tone resonating around the spacious room like a Gilbert and Sullivan rendition of the *Mikado*. 'Come along; I don't have all day.'

Shocked into a response, one spluttered, 'Jones, madam.'

'Smith, err, Lady Drakeford,' said his colleague.

I waited for the correction I knew to be coming.

'I see,' she began. 'Well, that will be easy to remember, and you almost got it correct.' HG pointed to the leaner of the two. 'Not Lady, Smith. Rather, Your Grace. As for you, Jones, you must purchase a copy of *Debrett's* if you wish to make anything of yourself.'

Smith and Jones exchanged uncomfortable glances as their ordeal continued.

'May I introduce Lord Norwood, brother of my late lamented husband, and Rex, my personal assistant.'

Whipple and I smiled meekly as we came to terms with our new stations in life.

'Now that we are all friends, may I offer you two a glass of whisky? It's an 1887 single malt, you know.' Without further ado, HG poured two generous measures of the precious liquid and encouraged the two men to down their drinks in one go.

'Excellent. I like a man who can take his drink. Another?' Again, HG failed to await their answer and poured two further large measures of the single malt. 'There's plenty more where that came from, so don't be shy,' said the dowager. 'I've rubbed off the mark the butler left on the decanter to spy on house visitors. Oldest trick in the book, that one.'

Smith and Jones appreciated HG's candour, although I noticed no such action as she filled their glasses.

'Lord Norwood, shall you imbibe?' It took Whipple a few seconds before he realised HG was talking to him, then eagerly accepted the offer. 'As for you, Rex, I'm sorry; I need you to be sober when I call on His Majesty this evening.'

Mention of the King had the fellows spluttering into their cut-crystal glasses as I acted out my disappointment in missing the Scottish gold.

I noticed that the dowager always asked a question when the men took a gulp of whisky, which I took to be a deliberate strategy to keep them on their toes. She also left Smith and Jones with the clear impression of owning not only the alcohol they so eagerly consumed but the building they sat in.

'Now, how may I assist you? After all, it's Sunday, so I imagine a task that cannot wait until tomorrow must be of some importance.'

Smith, being the bolder of the two, announced that

since they were in the area, they thought it polite to call in on their good friend.

'How nice,' replied HG in a tone I likened to a spider observing its net for lunch. 'So good to have dependable friends, don't you think? However, as I mentioned, it's Sunday, and you are both in work attire. May I ask what line of business you are in?'

Again, Smith led their responses. 'Insurance services, Your Grace.'

'Insurance,' responded HG as she closed in on her quarry. 'How fascinating and I'm sure you're both most skilled in the endeavour. Tell me, do you specialise in domestic or commercial cover? I apologise if I sound knowledgeable; I'm not, though I have a family member who has something to do with Lloyds of London. One of my relatives started the business in the seventeenth century. In a coffee house of all things, would you believe it?'

'Life assurance,' said Smith, clearly watching what he said.

'How useful,' commented HG before filling their whisky glasses for a third time.

As they both began to gently rock from side to side, Jones asked when their friend might be available to meet with them, though the slurred nature of the man's speech made it increasingly difficult to interpret his words.

Whipple's alter ego, Lord Norwood, stepped forward and spoke in an ill-advised toff accent HG seemed to find amusing. 'We shall arrange the meeting immediately.' Turning to me, he added, 'Rex, 'I doubt you'll tear Morgan Prescott away from Willows and Jenkins. Perhaps all three might call in and say hello.'

I knew immediately to what the inspector referred and

left the room, glancing back at Smith and Jones to find them exchanging furtive glances.

Within ten minutes, mission accomplished, I re-entered the library with two police constables standing directly behind me.

Sight of the uniformed men caused Smith and Jones to jump to their feet, which I considered no easy feat given the volume of single malt they'd imbibed.

Before they could move, Inspector Whipple presented his warrant card with a flourish. 'I don't know what you two are up to, but I'll find out. Cuff them both, secure the windows and guard the doors from the outside until I return.'

12

A FINE SUIT

The corridor felt crowded as inspector Whipple stood outside the library doors and busied himself arranging the two constables while HG and I watched on as the police went about their work. 'Keep those doors locked. No one is to go into that room until I return. Am I understood?'

'Yes, sir,' responded the two officers in unison, eyes front, standing to attention.

Whipple's decisive action left me puzzled concerning what he'd do next. His declaration that he would check Smith and Jones out with Scotland Yard answered that question and for once, it was he who led and HG who followed.

Hardly had our progress begun when the colonel appeared from the dining room and waddled toward us in formal dress like a penguin making its way to water.

'What the devil is going on, Eleanor? The butler is all of a do-dah over some nonsense about bowler hats and making a nuisance of himself with the gravy boat. Lady Brentwood has set about the man for covering her shoulder, instead of the duck, with plum sauce. And now I see we have police officers standing guard. Are my library books really that important?'

HG's body language spoke to her command of the situation as she stood ramrod straight and moved forward three paces, forcing our host to give ground. 'Now, now, calm down, Colonel,' she began. 'The chief inspector has everything under control. It's a simple matter of two gentlemen who attempted to gain entry to the house for reasons I do not yet understand.'

Yet again, the dowager taught me a lesson in taking command. This time to control the situation in such a way that bent others to one's own will.

'Bounders,' cried the colonel. 'Let me at them and I'll show those unctuous fellows what it means to cross a senior officer of His Majesty's Eleventh Hussars, retired. Keep them incarcerated while I fetch my sabre. I shall soon have them talking. Do you hear?'

Unlike the alarm Whipple showed, HG remained calm. She reminded the colonel that it wasn't the done thing to run through one's visitors with a sword.

Playing to the ex-military man's sense of fair play did the trick. 'Very well, Eleanor. I see your point. In that case, I shall leave matters in the capable hands of the inspector and return to my duck before the butler suffers further injury from Lady Brentwood.'

Just as I thought events could not deteriorate further, Augustine made her presence known.

HG attempted to head matters off. 'There is no need for further agitation. Inspector Whipple is about to check the intruders' identities with Scotland Yard and arrange police transport to the local station.'

'But who are the fellows?' asked Augustine.

'A couple of tricksters,' responded the inspector.

'How wonderful,' replied our host. 'Are they employed in one of those bohemian travelling circuses? I wonder what sort of tricks they do. I love magicians, don't you, Eleanor? Do you think they might perform one or two illusions for us all after dinner?'

After closing both eyes, the colonel shook his head and scratched his furrowed forehead with a curled finger. 'I'm sure Eleanor will ask them. In the meantime, perhaps we ought to get back to our other guests?'

'Very well, I'll pop in to welcome them to our home. I'm sure they'd enjoy tea and a piece of cake, don't you?'

As Augustine made for the library doors, I sensed the inspector raising his hand to bar her way.

HG again showed her diplomatic skills. 'Not to worry, dear; I've made sure they're being well looked after. Now, off you go back to dinner. The duck sounds excellent.'

Augustine smiled while brushing her hair back with a hand and taking a keen interest in a fly being bothersome to the inspector. 'Very well. I shall arrange things with cook.'

The colonel shook his head again as Augustine sauntered down the corridor and disappeared. 'She hasn't always been like this, you know,' said the colonel to no one in particular. 'Never the same after a Zeppelin raid on London in 1915. She got caught smack in the middle of it all, poor woman.' A few seconds of silence fell as the colonel's words sank in. 'Never mind, we must carry on. That's the thing to do. Battle through and all that.'

I detected the slightest glistening of the old officer's eye before he quickly gathered his wits and made for the dining room.

'A question, Colonel. Can you remind me of the quickest way to the kitchen? I wish to see how my girl is doing.' At first, HG's question seemed obtuse, not to say unusual.

However, all became clear when our host obliged the dowager before waddling back to the dining room, looking more like a penguin than ever from the rear.

'But you know where the kitchen is,' said the inspector. 'It's down there and down the stairs to the left.'

'Yes,' replied the dowager, but Augustine turned to the right.'

———

Leaving the inspector to call for police transport and check Smith and Jones' alibi, HG declared it time to change direction, resulting in the two of us setting off for the butler's pantry. 'I bet he's hiding there before supervising the dining room tidy-up and serving after-dinner drinks.'

Sure enough, as we descended from the ornate decor of the main rooms into the monotone cream world of the servant's working area, the gentle sound of a man snoring permeated the primary service corridor below stairs.

When we reached the butler's pantry, a small room next to the housekeeper's office, both of which lay next to the kitchen, Lomas was asleep in a rocking chair. The small section of clear glass in the top two panels of the pantry door allowed only limited vision into the pantry's interior, though it proved sufficient for our purposes.

'You know the glass is only there so he might monitor the comings and goings of staff,' said HG. 'No one would dare engage in eye contact with him if they sensed the butler watching them. A good control measure, do you not think?'

I knew perfectly well that the dowager would never allow such devious means to observe staff about their business in her own houses, so left her question unanswered.

'Let's be about our business,' she said before opening the pantry door as quietly as possible.

The glass in the door failed to hide much, for all that the room contained, other than the butler in repose, was a small wooden table and two chairs; walls lined with shelves, on which stood a variety of cleaning instruments, some of which might well have seen service in the Tower of London's dungeons; and an iron bar gate, securely locked, leading to the wine cellar and silver strongbox.

I was directed by HG to lift a great iron key from a rusty nail sunk into the wall, when mention of the wine cellar roused the butler from his slumber. 'Wine... what are you... who are...? Oh, Your Grace. May I assist?'

The dowager once again turned on the charm. 'My apologies for disturbing you. I know your working day to be a long one, but I thought it important we discussed reported shortages in the wine inventory.'

The news was as shocking to me as it was the butler, whose eyes were open so wide as if held by matchsticks.

With colour draining from Lomas' face at an alarming rate, I assumed HG had perchance come upon vital information she'd chosen not to share with me.

Lomas protested that his ledger received the colonel's attention each week and its reconciled contents was signed off by his employer. 'There is no discrepancy between what is in my ledger and what rests on those shelves.' Lomas pointed to a point beyond the iron gate.

HG's malign smile signalled she was onto the man. 'I'm more interested in the real ledger, not the work of fiction you put before the colonel.'

Now on his feet, if a little unsteady from his recent snooze, the butler remonstrated with the dowager. 'Your

Grace, I shall have no alternative but to inform my employer of your, if I may say so, scurrilous assertions.'

The dowager broke into a burst of quite raucous laughter as she bade me hand over the great iron key. 'We both know it's the last thing you'll do, for any auditor worth their salt will reveal your fraud within thirty seconds.'

HG told the fellow that unless he gave satisfactory answers to the questions she had for him, then she'd inform the colonel, adding, 'And, of course, new positions are so scarce without satisfactory references, don't you agree?'

Waiting with bated breath to discover what might happen next, I watched the butler as his shoulders slumped and he directed that we each take a chair.

'That's better,' commented the dowager. 'Let us begin. I'm interested in the accident the old head gardener suffered some years ago.'

Lomas made the mistake of denying knowledge of such an accident.

'Very well, Mr Lomas, then we're done here. I'm sure the colonel will require your presence and explanation in a short while.'

Before we got to our feet, the butler extended a hand to show we might remain. 'You must consider the fact I held the position of second footman, so what I tell you now comes from staff gossip.'

'Continue,' replied the dowager, leaning forward with all the charm of an eagle waiting to pounce.

'Everyone said their son, Peregrine, did it. But all said it to be an accident. In fact, thinking back, everyone I spoke to offered me the same explanation.'

HG closed in. 'Then you know more?'

'Years later I spoke to the poor gardener, you know, when

my station here allowed me to do such things without getting a clip around my ears. Well, he told me what happened. The only other thing I know is that they sent their son away soon after. He didn't return for a couple of years but he's a bad'un alright. Just stands there, watching. Always watching.'

The dowager relaxed her frame and even offered the butler the semblance of a smile. 'Where was the wretched boy sent?'

Lomas shrugged his shoulders. 'They palmed him off to a minor prep school in Yorkshire. He wasn't there long; got expelled for hurting another boy. I don't mean only bashing the lad, I mean a proper pasting.'

'And then?' asked HG.

'Then to a junior army officers academy. I remember the boy crying when he came home for the holidays, but they always sent him back. I imagined they believed army discipline kept him in check.'

Curious, I asked if the boy hit anyone while undergoing training.

The butler intoned that Peregrine was a coward, soon backing down if challenged, so no, he kept his head down there. Lomas then said something troubling. 'The army controlled him, but also trained him. Now he's more disciplined, sneakier... and more dangerous if you ask me. Put it like this. I wouldn't want to cross the man.'

At this point, I expected the dowager to ask for additional information. However, she settled back into her chair for a moment, offered Lomas a broad smile and said he could now return to his slumber in peace.

'The ledger?' said Lomas, concern etched on his face.

'You need not concern yourself about that matter. All shall remain confidential, though I would advise that you move the key from its current location. After all, we simply walked in and removed it from the wall. Should anyone wish you harm, you allow them the easiest of opportunities to prove your, how shall I put it... eccentric accounting methods.'

Once back in the service corridor, I could contain my enquiries no longer. How did the dowager know Lomas kept two sets of books?

'I didn't,' exclaimed the dowager. 'He merely looks the type. I expect he keeps the real ledger in the silver strong-box; they always do. Only the butler and master of the house keep keys to the strongbox. I assume Lomas knew the possibility of the colonel bothering to check up on his butler so remote it was not worth bothering about.'

———

LEAVING HG TO ATTEND WHAT REMAINED OF DINNER, I SPENT my time attempting to calm the inspector, who

se incessant pacing of the colourful tiles in the hallway, waiting for police transport to arrive

PRESENTED A DANGER HE MIGHT WEAR AWAY THE GLAZE beneath his feet.

'Intolerable,' grunted Whipple as he looked out of a large window onto the gravel drive for the umpteenth time. 'We shall check up on Smith and Jones, if only to waste a little time.'

Before the two constables realised what was happening, Whipple was upon them and chiding both for their slovenly appearance. 'Do you think it would impress His Majesty were it he, and not me, who now stood before you?'

I assumed the two men could not make a suitable

response so instead patted their tunics down, adjusted the chin strap of their helmets and kept their eyes resolutely to the front.

'Unlock this door. I have no time for lazy officers, and this isn't the last time we shall speak of this.'

Fumbling to turn the key, so anxious was one constable that he dropped it onto the carpet.

'Get out of my way,' shouted Whipple. This was an unpleasant side of the inspector I had not seen before.

Having flung the library doors wide open, the inspector stood for a moment, mouth wide open, eyes flitting from place to place. 'They're gone. the room is empty. What is the meaning of this? Did you not check on your prisoners?'

PC Willows calmly responded. 'But you told us not to go in, sir?'

I thought the inspector about to explode. 'I said not to let anyone in until I returned. That did not include you... or you.'

The second constable remained busy looking at a painting on the opposite wall of the corridor to avoid eye contact with his superior.

Whipple's eyes narrowed as he turned his attention back to PC Willows. 'Remember what I said about that red flag, and I don't give tuppence if the law no longer exists. I ordered you to secure the windows, so how come one is wide open?'

'I did, sir,' responded the PC with, I thought, a touch too much attitude. 'There was that much paint on it, the thing wouldn't move.'

I awaited the inevitable with bated breath. 'Paint? You mean to tell me His Majesty's finest now rely on a coat of paint to secure prisoners? Give me strength. Get after them and don't come back until you find them, or else.'

There is much to be admired in obeying one's superior's orders, no matter what the consequence might be for the individual. Here, it pleased me to know the library was at ground level as the two officers pluckily clambered through the open window and disappeared into the extensive grounds belonging to the house.

I followed as the inspector stormed from the room and tore down the corridor, picking up a Laxton's Superb eating apple from a porcelain dish on a small round oak table in the centre of the hallway.

Striding impatiently from the front doors to supervise the search for Smith and Jones, the inspector came to a halt as a Daimler, driven by a man in a suit, pulled up on the gravel. An immaculately dressed man in a sharp pinstriped suit, complete with rolled black umbrella, climbed from the rear of the enormous car.

'You must be Chief Inspector Whipple of Scotland Yard, and I take it you're the ward of Eleanor, Dowager Duchess of Drakeford.'

I didn't know quite how to respond when Whipple leaned into me and whispered, 'Ward?'

I decided a shrug of the shoulders and a smile might suffice.

'Horizons Home for Foundlings. You were in there?'

Again, I offered a meek smile.

'I knew I recognised your face when I first saw you. Of course, you're a good bit older now.'

Before the inspector could delve into my background, the pinstriped man interjected. 'Touching though this reunion is, I should like to see the dowager at your early convenience, which, for the sake of clarity, means now.'

Just then, the inspector's men reappeared wearing wide smiles. One holding Smith, the other, Jones.

'Ah, this is a tad embarrassing, Chief Inspector. However, please order your men to release these two at once.'

Inspector Whipple looked far from pleased at this latest development. 'What... Who are you anyway?'

Pinstripe exhibited not the slightest sign of irritation as he repeated his instruction. 'Constables, remove their handcuffs if you would be so kind. The two gentlemen will await me in the rear of the Daimler. As for who I am, Inspector, that's not your concern for the present.'

Unsure what to do, both PCs looked to their superior officer for guidance. To my astonishment, Whipple simply nodded his head. Free of handcuffs, the sorry pair averted their eyes from Pinstripe and clambered into the back of his car.

'And now, the dowager, if you will.'

13

THE WATCHER

As the inspector and I accompanied the pinstriped stranger to the library, I asked Lomas to fetch the duchess. Our party exchanged not a single word until we reached the two PCs stationed outside the room, even though the prisoners rested in the back of a Daimler limousine.

'Apart from Her Grace, no one is to enter this room until I return. Do you understand, officers?' This time they didn't check the order with their direct superior, instead touching their police helmets to confirm their understanding while eyes remained resolutely to the front.

The suave gentleman waited for the doors to open before gliding effortlessly into its plush interior. Whipple and I exchanged baffled glances, wondering why this man oozed power yet showed no documentation to prove who he was or whom he represented.

By the time we three had selected a seat and settled into the plush leather upholstery the colour of a fine red wine, HG appeared at the doors looking her imperious best.

'Why are you here? What is it that concerns your endeavour?' If HG knew the fellow's name, she did not use it. It was clear from her facial expression that she knew Pinstripe well, and I assumed she had a perfectly valid reason for keeping the chap's identity secret.

'So nice to see you again, Eleanor. May I say you look splendid tonight.' Pinstripe's failure to answer HG's question puzzled me; these were two people who appeared to have a history, yet all the warmth of an iceberg with flu flowed between them.

For the next five minutes, they verbally toyed with each other, which, to an outsider, might sound and look like a perfectly amiable series of exchanges. However, I recognised HG's guard was up, meaning she'd not give one inch of ground.

It never ceased to amaze me that such people might exchange the gravest of insults without breaking their smiles or raising voices.

In my early years, I spent much time among actors and other theatrical types who would think nothing of sabotaging their rival's performance then resorting to Anglo Saxon insults and fisticuffs when challenged.

Pinstripe's next question to HG showed that their playful exchanges had ended. 'What do you know of Morgan Prescott?' His move from genial guest to threatening visitor appeared so effortless it seemed even more sinister. Who was this man?

HG waved a hand as if removing a fly from her immediate vicinity. 'In truth, little. We discovered the unfortunate fellow in the lake, or at least that bit which remained above water; his arm, in fact.'

So far, every word the dowager spoke was a faithful

reflection of events. Yet Pinstripe's response was to smile in the manner of the Mona Lisa.

'Excellent,' he replied. 'Then it will be of no trouble to you, in fact, to you all, that his presence must be erased him from your collective memories.' Again, the fellow spoke in that same quiet, self-assured tone so often displayed by men of a certain class who spent their formative years at preparatory school, then Eton, Rugby or one of the few other top-notch public schools.

'This is a police matter. I'll ensure Scotland Yard does no such thing.' Inspector Whipple's tone was firm and lacked any of the refinement of his opponent yet rendered his authority clear to all.

Pinstripe lowered his head the smallest fraction while positioning his eyes at a slight upward angle as he genially smiled at a rattled Whipple. 'No, it isn't, Chief Inspector; it's my concern. Let us not argue the point since I know you have other fish to fry before the colonel's guests depart tomorrow morning. Let this be, Inspector. It will be better for all concerned.'

Whipple chose not to concur. 'Then I shall contact my superior and see what he has to say.'

It was as if the inspector had sprung Pinstripe's trap. 'There really is no need,' he began. 'I have already done so. The commissioner was quite understanding, especially when I informed him the home secretary was desirous of such an outcome.'

The stranger's response left Whipple dumfounded as he glanced at HG for inspiration.

'It is how this gentleman operates,' said the dowager, over-emphasising the word 'gentleman'. 'Unfortunately, you must believe what he says.'

I watched Pinstripe smile with satisfaction as he reclined into his deeply buttoned leather seatback. It was at this point he changed the direction and tone of the conversation on its head. Gone was the quiet threat. Now his tone reflected life-long friends catching up after too long apart. 'And how is the family, Eleanor?'

HG resumed her countenance of a refined duchess as she played his game. 'My son now runs the estate and I live in the smaller of our two country houses, Drakeford Old Hall.'

Satisfied with her response, he then turned his attention to me, which I found most uncomfortable. 'It's been what, six years since Her Grace took you under her charitable wing, so to speak? Was it not fortunate your father saw fit to leave you at the doors of Horizons as a youngster, before he died in debtors' prison, I mean?'

Knowing from my body language I was about to bite back, HG stepped in on my behalf. 'You know only too well that his father was a great Shakespearean actor and mimic. You also know who tricked him out of his fortune.'

Their exchange triggered an anger I thought I'd long since put behind me. 'You knew my father?' I demanded.

Back came that enigmatic smile, which I was quickly learning to despise. 'I may have seen the gentleman upon the London stage on one or two occasions. His performances were certainly most competent.'

I realised since I spent most of my time watching from the wings when Father was on stage, the refined thug now sat opposite me may have been in the audience on one such occasion.

'Being the legal ward of a titled lady must have its advantages, yes?'

Again, HG took the lead to prevent me from disgracing

myself. 'That will do; enough of your insidious remarks. It diminishes you.'

For the first and only time during our meeting, I observed Pinstripe's eyes flash at HG. She had hit a nerve. However, the man instantly recovered his composure. 'As perceptive as ever, Eleanor. Oh, I'm sorry, I mean Your Grace.'

The inspector continued to observe the exchanges, wearing a look that flicked between bemusement and disbelief.

Pinstripe looked across to the whisky decanter, which HG also observed. 'Would you like a drink?'

'So kind, Your Grace. What vintage might it be? As you know, I only imbibe pre-1875.'

This was the first direct reference to the two, antagonist and protagonist, knowing each other on a personal level.

'Don't be so pompous, man. Is it to be whisky or a glass of water?'

Again, Pinstripe smiled that smile. 'Water, now there's a novelty. I'll have champagne instead.'

By now HG had run out of patience. 'You continue to spout nonsense. See to yourself if you require whisky from the decanter. Otherwise, you may take yourself off and seek the butler to fulfil your spirit requirements. Now, what do you want of us, other than to suffer a collective bout of amnesia?'

Pressing on the arm of his chair, Pinstripe eased himself to his feet. 'My colleague will, by now, have spoken to every member of this household, whether family, guest or servant. They now believe Morgan Prescott to have been a fraud who met his end through drink. Although sadly no longer with us, Mr Prescott remains of interest to us.'

Unable to contain his countenance further, the inspector

demanded to know who 'us' referred to. Pinstripe grinned this time. 'Oh, just 'us'. Well, I must be going.'

'By train again?' asked HG.

His grin morphed into a laugh. 'By motorised road vehicle, Eleanor, so you've no need to hide behind a porter's trolly this time.' The man's statement astounded me. We'd been under observation all the time.

With a lazy wave of his right hand, the man left, leaving the two police constables to peer into the room attempting, I suspect, to make sense of events.

Closing the door on his subordinates, Whipple asked HG if she knew who the fellow really worked for.

'For a government department that does not officially exist,' came her stark response. 'He specialises in recruiting intelligent, but naive, young men and women with access to diplomatic circles. Let us just say they are at first encouraged, then later required, to gather certain sensitive information which may be of use to His Majesty's government.'

HG's clarification stunned Whipple and me, prompting the inspector to seek further information. 'Encouraged... required. Do you mean he blackmails them?'

HG gave a wistful smile. 'Perceptive as ever, Arthur. Pinstripe exploits their weaknesses. It might be a lady's dalliance with an unsuitable gentleman, perhaps a man's betting habit. It matters not to our friend. The crux of the matter is that he exploits this weakness first with apparent kindness and willingness to 'help'. Once he has the unfortunate soul under his spell, they end up meeting his every demand. When they can do so no more... well, the terror of being exposed and banished from society is sometimes enough to drive them to the edge of a precipice from which they may not return.'

———

As we entered the drawing room, Pinstripe's declaration concerning his colleague lay revealed before us. The atmosphere was sullen with all eyes fixed upon us as we progressed into the centre of the silent space.

'Then you've been got at, have you?' I took HG's words to be more of a statement than a question.

No one answered. In fact, nobody moved a muscle, other than the colonel who puffed on his cigar contentedly. 'Would you believe it, the fellow breezed in, accused Prescott of being a chancer who must disappear from our recall, then vanished. Most ungentlemanly if you ask me.'

I noticed the dowager shift her attention to Augustine, who sat happily twirling her hair with a finger as she perused her *Vogue* magazine.

'Dear Augustine, might you have any insight into the matter?'

The colonel's wife, who seemed immersed in an article, eventually looked in the general direction of HG. 'Insights, dear? I don't wear them. Why would I need such things since I can walk perfectly well without such aids?'

Shaking his head, the colonel removed his huge cigar and spat out an errant flake of tobacco leaf. 'No, dear; insights, you know, knowledge. Not insteps. Do pay attention.'

Augustine gave a whimsical smile and apologised to the dowager for misunderstanding, pointing to her magazine. 'Such a fascinating piece on a delightful new evening ensemble by Gabrielle Chanel.'

Following the brief interlude of conversation, the room fell quiet again until the ever-avuncular colonel suggested a game of cribbage.

My heart sank, since I had always found the pursuit baffling, especially the scoring system. 'Fifteen-three, fifteen-four, fifteen-five and three is eight', or some other such number, seemed to be an overcomplicated means by which to determine if a person had won a game.

Inspector Whipple clearly shared my view as he left, citing urgent business as his reason. This left the colonel and HG to organise the room, which, following their instruction, broke into two groups and settled around allotted tables, while the butler and a footman retrieved sufficient playing equipment from a cupboard to meet everyone's needs.

Thankfully, after approximately ten minutes of trying to keep up, my salvation came from a faint knock on one of the beautiful white painted and gilded doors to the drawing room.

As the butler opened one leaf of the twin-doors, I glimpsed Mable Popkiss, HG's cook. Being protective of the young lady, I became concerned with the expression on her strained face. Seconds later, and without allowing Mable to enter, Lomas walked across the room as if processioning before His Majesty. Leaning forward, he whispered into HG's ear.

The dowager rose immediately and signalled I should follow. Closing the door behind us, we now stood in an elegant corridor decorated in the Regency style, with a row of painted family portraits lining each wall.

'A man has been watching me almost since we arrived,' said Mable.

HG immediately arrived at her view on the matter. 'That Peregrine fellow. I shall have his ears off.'

Seeing Mable becoming upset, the dowager put her arms around her. How I wished it was I giving Mable comfort. 'Don't worry, Mable,' said HG. 'We shall find the man and put a stop to it. You have my word.'

It surprised me when Mable shook her head. 'No, it's not him. I haven't had an unobstructed view of his face, but it's not the colonel's son, I'm sure of it.'

Mable's announcement flummoxed us. If not Peregrine, who had a well-earned reputation for his voyeurism, then who? As the three of us sat on a long, delightfully upholstered bench seat, I asked Mable to repeat what she'd told me earlier about being watched early the previous day after breakfast. 'I saw a man looking through the kitchen window at me,' said Mable. 'He wore a riding hat with the peak covering most of his face. Then, later in the afternoon when I went for coal from the store in the courtyard, he was looking at me again. The last time was an hour since. I was in the scullery; the kitchen was empty. I got the feeling of being watched. It was horrible.' Mable broke down again.

'There, there,' said HG as she drew Mable into her. 'You have a rest until you're ready to carry on.'

It took only a few seconds for Mable to sufficiently recover to complete her report. 'I turned around. I didn't see him, but I know he was there, feet from where I stood.'

The dowager took hold of Mable's hand and began to gently stroke it. 'But how can you be so sure someone was there?'

Mable slowly placed her left hand into her starched, white apron, before holding up a folded piece of paper. 'It's a poem. He wrote me a poem. I found it on the floor where he'd stood.'

HG read the short poem aloud. Whoever penned the stanza clearly felt the deepest affection for the lady, be it Mable or another.

As the words sank in, HG posed Mable a question. 'If we

are to find this fellow, I need your help. You will need to be brave. Do you think you can?'

Confused at first, Mable drained of colour as HG explained her plan. Mable would need to act as bait to allow HG and me to spring our trap.

———

ENCOURAGING MABLE TO GO BACK TO THE KITCHEN, HG assured her that I'd be close on the tail and that neither of us would allow anything to befall her.

'I'll check which men are absent from the cribbage tables. That, at least, might give us a clue who we are up against,' said HG as I followed Mable down the corridor.

As Mable transited from the sumptuous decor of the ground floor down into the staff work areas, I maintained a close watch for anyone who looked out of place in the main thoroughfare used by staff to move supplies and services between the quite different worlds of servants and employers.

At twenty-one, I knew things were changing and that the deference shown by one class to another had loosened because of the Great War. But I thought too many differences remained. Mable being frightened by the possibility of a toff taking advantage of a servant struck me as one such example.

Bravely, Mable did as HG asked and acted within the confines of the kitchen as if nothing were amiss, first tidying one pile of plates away, then hanging the great copper cooking pots back onto their allotted hooks. I did, however, watch Mable hesitate before lifting the galvanised metal coal scuttle and making her way to the rear door of the kitchen, which led out into the dark courtyard.

Just as Mable exited the door, HG appeared at my shoulder to say both Peregrine and Lemuel Norris were missing from the room. Momentarily distracted by the dowager's arrival, I was several seconds behind Mable's progress. A piercing scream from the courtyard told me it was a few seconds too many.

As HG and I rushed into the dark quadrangle, there was little to see at first. Once our eyes adjusted to the conditions, we saw Mable sat on the cobbled floor, the coal scuttle several feet away.

Rather than in tears, it was a furious Mable that presented herself to us. 'I threw it at him,' she said, pointing to the dented scuttle. 'He'll have a bruise alright; I caught his elbow. It must have hurt because it landed with a heck of a wallop. Do you know, he didn't murmur a word; he ran for it. Sorry, I didn't see who it was.'

It was then HG asked what I thought a peculiar question. 'Did he have any fingers missing from his right hand?'

The question appeared to baffle Mable since her response amounted to such a thing might have been possible but it was too dark to know.

I whispered to HG that I'd assumed we were concentrating on the two absent men from the drawing room. The dowager confirmed as much, before reminding me the farrier had commented on the poacher spending a great deal of time on the estate.

Having dispatched Mable to her bed with the promise of a few days off when we returned to Drakeford Old Hall, we surveyed the quadrangle for a few minutes before HG determined we should return to the other guests and observe if either Peregrine or Lemuel had also returned.

We didn't have to wait long for an answer. As we crossed back from the servants' area to the ground floor via a jib door, we watched Lemuel Norris crossing the hallway on his way to the drawing room. As he did so, Lemuel continually rubbed his elbow.

14

A SECRET MEETING

'Ah, there you are,' said HG as Inspector Whipple knocked and entered through the door to the dowager's sumptuous bedroom.

Hardly had he sat down on one of three delightful Regency upholstered chairs when he launched into his report. 'The pinstriped one may think he's clever, but no one gets the better of Scotland Yard. I called in a few favours and it turns out Messrs Smith and Jones are really Samuel Finch and Raymond Crown, or at least that's the most recent names we have for them. They're a couple of two-bob chancers that appear then vanish from police files. Then we catch them again with alternative names.

I asked the inspector how he discovered their true identities.

'The old files get archived, but a mate in the records department recognised my descriptions and did some digging. They work for the highest bidder but can't help themselves from a little "private work" i.e., housebreaking, which they're not proficient at, hence we continue to catch them.'

I commented it appeared to confirm they had friends in high places. HG corrected my calling them friends instead of handlers, and said that they were no simple house-breaking team.

'No matter,' continued HG, 'we must tell Arthur all about Mable.' Her reference to the cook caused Whipple to frown.

'... And then Rex and I came upon Lemuel rubbing his elbow. A little coincidental, don't you think? And so, it leaves Peregrine to track down to check what he's been up to recently,' said HG.

After the arduous climb to the top of the house, our reward amounted to a room without an occupant. Despite several sharp knocks on the dingy door, there came no answer. Kneeling to check the keyhole, I found it to be clear, meaning either the man removed the key from the inside and was now hiding in a corner, or Peregrine was not in the room at all. We agreed the latter to be the case and began our descent of the steep stairway, which felt much easier than the earlier ascent.

As we cleared the landing on the second floor and embarked on the final thirteen steps, Lemuel Norris came from the opposite direction, head down and moving at pace.

As the man passed us, for some extraordinary reason, which I did not understand for several seconds, Inspector Whipple stumbled into Lemuel, as if about to fall. Apolo-gising profusely, the inspector touched Lemuel's right arm as if to steady himself. At this point, Lemuel let out a cry of pain and grabbed his elbow.

'I'm sorry if I've injured your arm, Mr Norris,' said Whipple. Is it very painful? Perhaps I may look?' Lemuel immediately shrank back, thanked the inspector for his concern and hurried up the stairs.

HG turned to us both. 'We have to get a look at that elbow.'

Deciding to avoid exposure to the cribbage tournament, we sauntered to the peaceful solitude of the colonel's smoking room. A relatively small space for such a big house, the room enjoyed a pervading fragrance of fine Havana cigars. On a low table between a matching pair of Chippendale chairs sat a low, round mahogany table with an ironed copy of the *Sunday Times* resting upon it.

'This will do nicely,' announced HG as she sat on a burgundy-coloured upholstered bench seat that hugged a delightfully proportioned stone bay window. She suggested the inspector might like to pour three sherries from a decanter resting behind the framed glass door of a display cabinet while intertwining her fingers, meaning a question would soon follow.

'Let me ask you both something,' said HG as she looked out over the moonlit landscape. 'Is it possible someone has deliberately diverted us from Ambrose Bagley's death, courtesy of Morgan Prescott's demise?'

Each taking a sip of sherry gave Whipple and me time to think on the matter and construct a half-sensible response. I knew from experience that HG expected full attention to all she said and expected an intelligent, well-considered reply.

'You mean Pinstripe?'

'You answer a question with a question, Rex, which isn't helpful now.'

I noticed that HG's mild reprimand made Inspector Whipple wince. About to speak, he took another sip of his sherry.

I tried again. 'What I meant to say is assuming Pinstripe is behind this whole thing, Ambrose is the key to events, not

Morgan.' Pleased with my second attempt, I awaited HG's pleasure.

'Better, Rex. Much better,' she replied while winking to confirm her pleasure at the apprentice learning his trade.

Meanwhile, Whipple rolled one of the colonel's Havana cigars he'd liberated from a silver case on the small round table. 'I bet these were a pretty penny,' he mused while passing the tightly wrapped tobacco under his nose to drink in each note's bouquet.

'And the answer to my question, Arthur?' asked HG impatiently.

'Ah, yes, I've considered your ward's theory. What if Pinstripe is playing a game of double bluff? What if he wants us to believe Morgan Prescott was a tragic pawn in the fellow's game when it was, in fact, Ambrose?'

HG and I frowned at one another. 'Is that not what Rex said? Really, Arthur, I wish you'd concentrate instead of drooling over the colonel's Havanas.'

Whipple appeared hurt at HG's chastisement, turning to the cigar for comfort. 'All I'm—'

'Good heavens,' announced HG, staring at a Charles II timepiece on the mantle. 'Look at the time; I said I'd call in on Mable to see how she is. Come, we must depart for the servants' quarters.'

I attempted to gently remind HG that men could not enter the female servants' quarters under any circumstances. 'And who shall argue the point with me, pray?' HG replied as she raced past Whipple and me.

I detected the inspector felt a sense of loss at having to put the cigar back into its silver case but thought all the better of him for upholding the honour of his office by fighting the temptation to filch it.

As the door from the service corridor up to the female

sleeping quarters neared, I felt a bead of perspiration forming on my brow. Looking back on Whipple, I noted he had already taken to mopping his forehead with a cotton handkerchief.

'Are you sure this is a good idea, Your Grace?'

HG turned on me. 'Don't you start that "Your Grace" with me; it won't wash. A promise is a promise, and you'll both do as you're told.'

———

AS WE CLIMBED THE WOODEN STAIRS, DESIGNED TO CREEK SO that it might undo male intruders, HG strode forth as if her life depended upon it. At last, we stood by Mable's door. After a gentle knock, the dowager opened the door and announced she'd brought a couple of friends as another female member of staff came out of her room, presumably having heard the creaking stairs.

Never have two men with almost forty years' age difference between them moved so quickly to escape the look of disgust that the lady gave us. Relieved to be inside the tiny room with the door shut, I looked upon Mable's smiling face.

'I'll be the talk of the house by breakfast; it's a good job we're off back to Drakeford tomorrow.'

Enjoying, it seemed, Whipple and my discomfiture at the turn of events, HG wore a smile broader than simply calling on her cook merited to my mind. She enquired after Mable's condition and, satisfied all appeared well, broadened the conversation out to ask if she had anything to report back on the 'little task' she gave Mable. Not knowing to what HG referred, Whipple and I looked at Mable with anticipation.

It seemed the dowager asked Mable to have a cup of tea with Augustine's lady's maid to determine if she might say anything pertinent to recent events she'd be unwilling to say to the police or HG.

'I was a little surprised she told me so much,' began Mable. 'After all, we don't know one another. Anyway, it seems she saw her mistress talking with a smartly dressed gentleman in the summer house. She didn't half go on about how expensive his suit was. Something about stripes.'

HG enquired how the maid came to be by the summer-house. 'On her way back from running an errand, she said, and took a shortcut across the grounds that took her right by the building.'

'Did they see her?' asked the inspector in a tone better suited to an interview room at Scotland Yard, and which earned the man admonishment from HG.

Mable shook her head. 'She says not, but she was in a hurry because it was already nearly ten and she had to get her mistress' nightclothes ready and turn down the bed.'

A knock on the bedroom door interrupted our discussions. As it opened, the stern face of the housekeeper appeared. 'And what are you two doing in... Ah, Your Grace, so sorry to interrupt, I—'

HG assessed the situation in an instant and turned on the charm. 'Thank you for doing your duty and checking up on my cook. You are a tribute to your station and the colonel will hear of your dedication to duty. I wonder, may we have a further few minutes with Mable?'

The housekeeper's stern features melted as she bathed in the comforting glow of a duchess' good favour. 'Of course, Your Grace. We shall say no more about this.' With that, she gave a well-practised curtsy, withdrew and quietly closed the door.

Having left matters for several seconds to make sure all remained quite outside Mable's bedroom, our discussions continued as the inspector asked if the lady's maid had heard anything of her mistress' exchange with the man.

'She said the man sounded angry, not that he shouted, but the maid said she can tell when upper-class people are angry.' Realising what she'd said, Mable glanced at HG, before they broke into a quiet giggle.

I asked Mable if she had anything else to say. 'The maid said all she heard the man say was something about a train ticket. It made little sense to her, or me. Same thing about the papers.'

'The papers?' said HG.

Mable said the fellow had scolded the maid's mistress for not telling him about the message, because that's what she got paid for.

HG fell quiet. I recognised the twiddling of her pearls signalling she had remembered something. 'Rex, have you still got that newspaper cutting I gave you? With all this nonsense with whom you two euphemistically call "Pinstripe", I'd forgotten about that scrap of paper we found on Ambrose Bagley.'

I have to say that HG was not the only one who'd forgotten. My mind raced as I tried to recall what I'd done with the tiny scrap. At length, it came to me. 'My wallet,' I exclaimed to the amusement of my companions.

Retrieving one of the few reminders I had of my father, I opened the tattered leather keepsake. In one of the many pockets, constructed especially for my father as part of a magic act he sometimes performed, I came across the fragment. I reminded myself of its contents by reading the entry out loud.

15

A COMING TOGETHER

Bircham Manor looked much different in the darkness as its sixteenth century black and white timbered frame stood proud against the soft light of a full moon. Maintaining our cover beyond the tree line, the inspector and I kept up a steady pace as we walked down to the water's edge.

I questioned Whipple's assumption that the poacher may have returned to the lake, since he left himself open to easy discovery and capture. After all, the waterway was an artificial construct of Capability Brown's design that remained confined to the estate grounds.

My companion remained confident of his strategy as the mirror-like waters came into view. At first, it seemed the inspector's hunch was about to pay off. The small boat we'd used on Friday was absent, and in the distance, something appeared to disturb the lake's calm demeanour.

'It's him,' said Whipple as the small mass moved position. 'We need to get closer; follow me.'

We began a slow progress behind the tree line with eyes

peeled to avoid standing on small dry branches that might give our presence away.

As we neared the object, I doubted our target was a boat at all, or that it ferried the poacher pitting his wits, and remaining fingers, against Razor-Gob. Yet still, the inspector persisted. Only when an owl cried out did the truth of the matter reveal itself. Startled by the Tawney, a Grey Heron took off from a floating log, causing the timber to bob up and down from the thrust of the winged giant's take-off.

'Well, I'll be...' Whipple's few words, spoken with a tinge of disbelief, summed up the situation perfectly. Not only did we not find the poacher, but we'd also wasted time haranguing a heron.

As we discussed what to do next, the crack of a trodden-on fallen branch pierced the silence. Exchanging knowing looks, we gingerly made off toward the noise. No mean feat given the conditions underfoot and density of the spiky dog roses and brambles.

We slowed to a snail's pace as the camouflaged form of something moving through the trees held our focus.

'Can you see anything?' asked the inspector, to which I responded it may well have been our man.

Sadly, the figure turned out to be a roe deer, which scooted away at great speed the second it picked up our scent. To see the compact animal dart with precision through the dense woodland confirmed why an animal with no natural preda-tors, save for humans, thrived in the English countryside.

A sense of dejection descended as two false alarms sapped our enthusiasm for woodland stakeouts and we listened out for anything that might betray the man's loca-tion. Then the sound of someone murmuring several yards away floated through the dense greenery. Given the chaotic nature of the trees and other vegetation, at first, it proved almost impossible to pin down from which direction the man's voice came.

There it was again, this time closer, the man's mood having clearly not improved as his cursing sounded redolent of a drunken crowd at a boxing match. Each taking cover behind two particularly broad tree trunks, we waited. The voice came ever closer until at last, a shadowy figure showed itself against what little moonlight filtered through the tree canopy.

There he stood, a rough dressed man in a long overcoat several sizes too large for him, his head covered with an oversized fedora.

'They adapt those coats by sewing in extra pockets to the inside for their ill-gotten gains,' commented the inspector as we watched the fellow crouching down, murmuring words not fit for polite company, before moving several yards and crouching down again.

'He's checking for rabbit warrens. Looks like they're all abandoned, so no rabbit stew for him tonight. Come on, let's get him.' Whipple moved forward, not getting far before he stumbled into a wayward dog rose and tumbled to the ground. A combination of his rapid descent and his own colourful language spooked the poacher, who took off hardly any slower than the roe deer.

'Get him,' exclaimed the inspector as he fought a losing battle with the woodland undergrowth, which appeared determined to hang on to its captive.

Taking care not to suffer the same fate, I set off toward the man, yet as the minutes passed, it became clear he'd escaped courtesy of his excellent knowledge of the topography.

Admitting defeat, I turned to retrace my steps back to

the inspector, only to see the sorry sight of Scotland Yard's best, limping through the undergrowth while continuing to pick dog rose thorns from his hands.

'I've had enough of these thorns. I want a cup of tea.'

Whipple sighed. 'Would you mind me joining you?'

Even if the inspector might now unwittingly play gooseberry, the thought of seeing Mabel again took the edge off my frustration at losing our quarry. After all, what if the chap held a vital piece of information that might help our investigations? It looked now that the opportunity to find out had escaped us.

The aroma of fresh bread being baked for the morning in the kitchen eased my disappointment at Mabel having retired for the night.

'It's gone eleven, you know, and she'll be up at five to get things ready for breakfast,' said the head cook as she relaxed in a rocking chair by an enormous black cast-iron cooking range. 'Anyway, why are you tramping dead leaves all over my clean floor? What have you two been up to?'

It was only then I noticed the trail of organic debris that trailed behind us. I told her the story of a poacher, who seemed to move at the speed of light, and why we needed to speak to the phantom fish tickler.

'Come with me,' said the cook with a broad smile. 'There's someone you should both meet.'

Intrigued, we both followed her into the courtyard and over to a small building next to the estate washhouse.

Opening the latch, the cook spoke softly. 'It's only me.'

'What's going on?' said the inspector.

The answer came as we entered what looked like a rubbish store that held all the things the family wanted rid of yet couldn't bring themselves to part with. In the far corner, the hunched figure of a man sat at an old table, eating cottage pie.

'This is my daft brother, Wilfred.'

The cook's revelation astounded both Whipple and me as we watched the man tucking into his hearty meal without acknowledging our presence for one second.

'You mustn't tell the colonel or his wife, mind; they wouldn't understand.'

When I asked what the cook meant, she explained that like many ex-servicemen, he'd fallen on hard times after coming back from the war and that losing two fingers to the pike hadn't helped matters.

'Though why he still poaches is beyond me when I feed him. Then again, he's always been the same, so I don't suppose he'll stop now.' The cook turned to her brother. 'Will, I've brought two gentlemen to talk to you. They'll do you know harm; they need your help.'

For the first time since we'd disturbed his meal, the poacher turned to look at us. 'He's a copper; I can tell,' said Wilfred, looking intently at the inspector.

To give Whipple his due, he didn't rise to the bait. Instead, he made clear his disinterest concerning the fellow's poaching habit. 'But a little bird tells me you saw a drunken man by the lake on Friday?'

At first, Wilfred refused to speak, instead taking several mouthfuls of his sister's cottage pie. However, after a gentle prod from her, the poacher put down his fork while shrugging his shoulders. 'It was one heck of a clout. He went down like a sack of spuds. He looked funny with his hand held out like that, but I doubt he know what hit him.'

The poacher's description confirmed the dowager's and my assessment of the rapid decline of Ambrose Bagley.

However, it was Wilfred's second declaration that put the cat among the pigeons.

'As for the other one, I didn't see what happened, but he was arguing with someone. The next thing I see is a drunken bloke wandering by the water and someone stood by the trees, just watching.'

I HADN'T SEEN INSPECTOR WHIPPLE SO ENERGISED BEFORE. 'I intend to search Peregrine and Lemuel Norris' bedrooms. One of them must have been there. Who knows, we might get lucky and find evidence that links one of them to Ambrose Bagley's death. Perhaps even Morgan Prescott's, no matter what Pinstripe said.'

For a man who looked near to his sixth decade, Whipple certainly knew how to move when the mood took him. Walking quickly from the courtyard into the kitchen, from where we transited the service corridor back upstairs via the jib door, it took only a further minute to reach Peregrine's bedroom.

'What if he's in there?' I asked, to which the inspector responded it addressed two issues in one go, since he also wished to interview the fellow.

As we opened the bedroom door and thanked our lucky stars it remained unlocked, it became clear Peregrine had not been back to his room since its being made up by the house staff after breakfast.

'Look for anything that might place him at the lake,' said Whipple as we began a methodical search of the room. The decor reminded me of a visit I once made to the botanical gardens in London. Not only did the wallpaper include representations of various flowers and leaf shapes, but several glass-fronted display cases adorned the walls and shelves, each containing an exquisite dried flower arrangement.

Other than that, and the furniture necessary to make the bedroom tolerably comfortable, the room contained no personal memorabilia denoting its usual occupant. It was as if an anonymous lover of the natural world inhabited the space.

Whipple went through a mahogany tallboy whose drawers become increasingly deep, one below the other. Taking his cue, I began a search of a bedside table comprising a small drawer and a cupboard. I found the latter to be empty, save for a King James Bible. The drawer contained nothing more interesting than a March 1921 copy of *The Garden Magazine*, which I took to be an American publication given the price on its front cover amounting to twenty-five cents.

As I gave the magazine a quick shake to see what might drop from its interior, Whipple remarked, 'And what have we here?'

Keen to establish what had caused the detective to ask the question, I turned to see him holding something within his handkerchief, a sure sign he thought the item to be evidence pertinent to our investigations.

Opening the material as I neared, he held a gold pocket watch, devoid of its chain. 'I consider this item as evidence that links the colonel's son to Ambrose Bagley's murder.'

'Shall we confront him now?' I asked.

Whipple shook his head, commenting that he wished to check one or two other matters first. The inspector added he wanted to give HG time to cogitate and come to her own conclusions before combining their intelligence. This, he said, was the way they'd worked together for several years and the extra time taken to do this always proved efficacious.

Next, the inspector wished to search Lemuel Norris' room to determine if Peregrine worked on his own, as the inspector thought, or if, despite their apparent hostility to one another, there might be some link between the two men.

We thought it to be too much to expect that his room might also be empty, and our assumption proved correct as a man in a smoking jacket and tartan slippers opened the door after Whipple's second knock.

'Can I help?' said Lemuel, to which the inspector replied he apologised for disturbing his evening but would appreciate a few minutes of his time.

Opening the bedroom door to its full extent, Lemuel invited us both in. His sleeping quarters turned out to be more luxurious than Peregrine's, which I put down to it being one of the formal guestrooms.

At first expecting Inspector Whipple to ask the man how his injured elbow was, I then realised he ignored the topic to see how our host conducted himself. However, I did not expect what followed.

'Mr Norris,' began the inspector. 'It is my view that you attacked Mable Popkiss, intending to compromise her person with your unwanted advances.'

Lemuel recoiled in shock and slumped into a bedside chair. Protesting his innocence, he demanded to know what evidence the detective held to form such a view.

Whipple pressed on. 'You stood behind that young woman earlier this evening as she went about her duties and dropped this.' The inspector withdrew a piece of paper from his inside pocket and waved it before Lemuel's pale checks. 'Do you deny this belongs to you?'

Still reeling from the verbal onslaught, Lemuel reached out to take the paper. His eyes scanned the stanza. 'Yes, this is mine, but I don't know how it came to be where you say you found it. I penned this to Rowena Dosett. She is the love of my life. Have you found the beast who accosted her?'

Whipple refused to relent. 'How do I know you didn't carry out the terrible deed?'

Lemuel, dumfounded, protested he could do the lady no harm. Astonishingly, the inspector then completely changed tack by asking the chap what his ambition in life might be.

The question threw Lemuel for several seconds, before he responded with what I thought an extraordinary answer. 'To fly.'

'Fly?' said Whipple.

'Imagine the freedom of being up in the sky, free of all earthly pressures, Inspector. Does that not sound a fine thing to do?'

'But isn't flying a tad dangerous?' responded the inspector. 'You know, what goes up must come down, that sort of thing?'

Then a second remarkable response from Lemuel, which I thought to be a joke. 'Not at all. What will be will be. If the worst happens, then I shall return in another form.'

I sensed the inspector's disbelief but marvelled at the professionalism he showed by continuing as if such talk the most natural thing in the world.

'And is your current form your first?'

'Of course not, Inspector; I can't remember all my reincarnations, of course, but two come to mind. First, my time as a frontiersman in Canada when the Hudson Bay Company behaved poorly to that country's indigenous inhabitants. The second concerns my period as a court jester to Elizabeth I at the time of the Spanish Armada.'

The inspector and I exchanged baffled looks while attempting not to belittle the fellow.

'You appear to have a thing about living through dangerous times?' said the inspector.

Undaunted, Lemuel ploughed on. 'My past lives mean I'm alert to danger and take all necessary steps to preserve—'

Whipple interrupted, 'Your life and freedom.'

'If you say so.'

The inspector shot back, 'Oh, I do, Mr Norris, and it's something that's currently at the front of my mind regarding your good self, I assure you.'

RETURNING TO HG'S ROOM, LEAVING SUFFICIENT TIME FOR cogitation, our attempt to gain entry failed as Whipple's repeated knock on the door went unanswered.

Only then did we hear a woman crying. Progressing slowly from one guestroom door to the next, we soon traced the source. The small rectangular name tag that sat within a brass frame on the door announced Miss Rowena Dosett as its occupant.

'What is a man to do?' commented the inspector as we hesitated over making our presence known for fear of being observed by someone and accused of entering a single lady's bedchamber.

As the seconds passed, our state of indecision worsened until, at last, we detected the voice of a second woman in the bedroom, and one we both readily recognised.

I echoed the inspector's sense of relief as we concluded it now safe to knock upon the door.

HG's imperious tone permeated the oak door to enquire, 'Who stands without? State your purpose or leave at once.'

Whipple risked a further quiet knock and announced who awaited her pleasure. After a few seconds, the door opened enough for us to see a tearful Rowena sat upon her bed, her head tilted downward.

'Here, take my key. I'll be along in a few minutes when I have this poor lady settled in bed.'

No sooner had I the key than Rowena's door closed again.

Returning to HG's room, we occupied ourselves by supping the colonel's best sherry and admiring the moonlit view from an exquisitely formed floor to ceiling bay window.

In the distance, the surface of the estate lake shimmered like a silver ribbon of diamonds, framed by a backdrop of intricate shapes as the trees danced in a light breeze.

As we forgot the sad events of the previous few days, the peaceful interlude soon evaporated as HR entered the room in a rare state of agitation.

'Poor Rowena, she remains so upset. I fear for her welfare if she cannot overcome that beastly attack. I have spoken to Dr Griffiths and he has agreed to administer a mild sedative to allow the woman a decent night's sleep. Let us hope her slumber has a restorative effect.'

Although the inspector and I both offered sympathetic noises, we wished to press on with more urgent matters as the time available to develop our plan for breakfast continued to shorten.

Furnishing HG with a sherry, the inspector briefed her

on the latest news of our investigations. The poacher, the watch in Peregrine's room.

Her Grace's demeanour changed to one of excited intellectual enquiry as she listed to Whipple's findings and our joint conclusions.

'I, too, have been busy, gentlemen. It may interest you to know, when I talked to the good doctor, he revealed the early findings of the post-mortems of Ambrose Bagley and Morgan Prescott.'

Our discussions on the ramifications of our joint discoveries and the various scenarios that now lay before us took more than an hour to distil.

As the clock on the bedroom mantle struck one o'clock, with which Whipple's and my own pocket watch agreed by chiming along, HR announced, 'Then we have our plan.'

16

ICED FANCY, ANYONE?

The dining room hummed with the hubbub of a dozen houseguests and their hosts as each stood in line at the breakfast buffet before taking their place at a long, elegant table covered with a crisp white cover and an assortment of silver condiments spaced evenly along its length.

HG, the inspector, and I hung back to ensure everyone had enjoyed their food before commencing our task. At length, the dowager approached the colonel at the head of the table and whispered into his ear.

After a nod of his head, our host rose to his feet. 'My friends, we've endured a tough weekend, from which no amount of tennis or horse riding, picnics or formal dining can distract. In that regard, may I crave your attention for Her Grace the Dowager Duchess of Drakeford, Chief Inspector Whipple of Scotland Yard, and... err, Her Grace's Person of all Works.'

I felt a roomful of eyes fall upon me, which made me wish I might explain my true station in life. However, now was clearly not the time for domestic matters.

Their interest in me soon waned as HG took centre stage

against the sumptuous backcloth of rich, dark oak wall panelling and sufficient silver to supply London's Hatton Garden for a year.

After completing the formal greetings as required by etiquette, the dowager offered a friendly smile to all, clasped her hands together and began her oration. 'When we all arrived on Friday, none could know of the tragedies to follow, and it's a testament to the colonel, and Augustine, that we have maintained a semblance of normality as the chief inspector has gone about his business with such diligence.'

Since clapping in such company is vulgar, all began to gently tap a hand on the table, accompanied by one or two 'Here-here's from various quarters.

'However,' continued HG. 'Very few people die, without cause especially fit, healthy young men. It is my belief, and when I say "my", I use it as a collective to include the good inspector, and my ward, Rex.'

Relieved my situation now rested in the public domain, as shown by several murmurs of surprise, I waited as the dowager allowed a few seconds for her audience to quieten down before recommencing.

'To continue, it is my belief that one, or both, of the gentlemen, did not meet their end by any natural cause. In short, murder stalks this place.'

The room erupted into chaos as some still eating almost choked on their food, while several guests spilt their cups of Twinings Morning Selection. The colonel got to his feet to enquire what the dowager meant.

'Colonel, I think my meaning clear. First, we discover a man lying dead in a most unusual horizontal position, then hours later, a second is spotted, or at least his raised arm, poking through the surface of your wonderful lake. It stretches one's imagination to consider either an entirely benign posture, wouldn't you agree?'

HG's infallible logic reduced the colonel to casting his eyes to the butler and barking for more tea, before sitting down and rearranging the knife and fork on his plate with a clatter.

Having patiently waited for our host to cease his fidgeting, the dowager pressed on. 'And so, we must ask ourselves the question, are we to look to one another for the identity of the murderer? Or did the perpetrator, or perpetrators, come from without, then vanish as if a malevolent spirit?'

'Oh, no, it's much too early for alcohol; I much prefer Twinings to tequila at this time of day.' A ripple of laughter filled the room as Augustine held forth, curling her hair around a finger, as usual, while chasing a troublesome cherry tomato around her plate.

'No, no,' began the colonel, before giving up his attempt to clarify the dowager's comment.

Now Inspector Whipple stepped into the fray, almost knocking off a Meissen porcelain figure of an elegantly dressed Regency lady playing a harpsichord, which sat on the mahogany sideboard he'd been leaning against. 'This is a mystery in which two men appear at first to be unrelated to each other's lives. Yet, through diligent police work, and yes, the skills of the noted amateur sleuth and police consultant, Her Grace the Dowager Duchess of Drakeford, and the impressive Rex, we now know those two unfortunate fellows were far from strangers to one another.'

Although not the gentlemanly thing to do, I felt a certain swell in my chest as the inspector acknowledged my part in the investigations.

'But surely one killed the other, then found he couldn't

live with what he'd done and did the decent thing by drowning himself?' said Watkins-Simms the elder.

'Nonsense,' remarked his younger twin. 'From everything the inspector has told us, the first chap, what's his name? Yes, Ambrose, well, he had a seizure and the other one, that Morgan Prescott fellow, he simply went for a swim without knowledge of Mr Bagley's death, and drowned. People forget how icy lake water is, even after a hot summer.'

Not to be outdone, the older twin re-joined the exchange. 'You always have to say the opposite to me. I'm sure if I concluded we were in for a fine day today, you would maintain a storm of biblical proportions imminent. Why can't you—'

'Gentlemen, please. Let's remember that two men are dead and our task this morning is to unmask the killer.'

HG's words stunned the twins into silence as a general gasp filled the refined air of the grand dining room.

'You suggest the murderer is in this room?' remarked the shocked colonel.

'We do,' replied the dowager.

'You see,' began Whipple. 'As Her Grace remarked to me on Friday, Oscar Wilde had something to say on the matter of not one but two similar events happening within a short amount of time. The issue here is that we are not attending a performance of his celebrated *The Importance of Being Earnest*. We are dealing in actual life, not a farce. Two men are dead, and justice must be served.'

At this point, Fredrick Blowers stood. 'But Inspector, did not a mysterious fellow threaten each of us with many disagreeable consequences if we chose not to forget Mr Morgan Prescott?'

Whipple eyed the man with suspicion. 'Ah, Mr Blowers,

so kind of you to remind us of that matter, yet this from a man who derided our other victim, Ambrose Bagley. What was it you said?' Whipple retrieved his police-issue notebook from an inside pocket of his jacket. 'Ah, yes, here we are. You characterised the deceased as a bounder and a cad, is that not so?'

The verbatim quote clearly unsettled Blowers, who fidgeted with his fob watch. 'But I explained the context of my words when you interviewed me. Why now do you recount only a partial element of my explanation?'

Whipple did not answer the question directly; in fact, he instructed the man to resume his seat and, instead, changed the subject. 'It's a fine fob watch that adorns your person, Mr Blowers. Do you collect such items of exquisite workmanship?'

Suddenly, all eyes focussed on the fellow's gold-plated timepiece. Blowers looked at the inspector as if attempting to form the words of a response.

Whipple didn't wait. 'Just an observation, Mr Blowers, nothing more, though I'll return to the subject of pocket watches in due course.'

His enigmatic words caused a further stir as one, then another, took a sip of tea, perhaps to distract themselves from a growing sense of threat pervading the room.

'As the chief inspector says,' began HG, 'words have consequences, intended or not. We've just heard an example. Did Mr Blowers intend his throw-away remark of a few days ago to be treated as a light-hearted jest? Or did his description of Ambrose Bagley point to a deeper hatred, perhaps even so heartfelt that it drove him to kill the man? However, we shall leave that matter be for a short while. Let us talk of Morgan Prescott.'

Blowers appeared to visibly shrink into his suit as his blood-drained features froze.

Taking care not to disturb the expensive Meissen figure a second time as he stood straight, the inspector picked up on the dowager's hint. 'Just how did Morgan Prescott come to be here in the first place? Well, the answer to that lies in a telephone call from Ambrose Bagley to the butler of this magnificent house.'

Lomas moved not a muscle as the inspector mentioned his name. Instead, the fellow continued to refresh a splendid silver teapot with boiling water from a hot water vessel of equal quality, heated from below by a paraffin burner.

'Ambrose asked Lomas if it were possible to furnish a room for one night to a certain Mr Prescott. This proves two things. First, that our two victims had a connection of some sort. Second, that Ambrose knew Morgan was coming. Why else go to the trouble of involving the butler?'

HG, itching to contribute to proceedings again, wandered over to the inspector's side. 'But what might that connection be? To answer that we must consider two crucial pieces of evidence. At first, a scrap of paper containing a reference to the Earls of Derby and a message in the personal column of a newspaper appear to have little in common.'

'Do you know Nelson's column, which stands proudly in Trafalgar Square, measures just under 154 feet and 3 inches tall? Quite remarkable when one thinks about it, especially since the man himself stood only five feet and one-half-inch.' Augustine's intervention caused less of a stir this time as everyone quickly returned their gaze to the dowager.

'What connects these two scraps of information? Let us look first at the reference on the scrap of paper.' HG held an arm out to me, which I at once realised called for that paper contained within my father's wallet. 'Two thirty, Earl of Derby, Haydock. Are we to believe Prescott had a meeting planned with the earl? Now, you might ask why are we so interested in this scrap? Well, it was found near the lake after the discovery of Morgan Prescott's murder.'

'It's a betting tip,' said Watkins-Simms the elder.

'I agree,' said the younger brother. Unexpectedly, the rare occurrence of the twins agreeing sparked a quick tapping of open palms on the dining table.

A genteel cough from the dowager was all it took to return the room to its previous state of concentration. 'Quite correct, sir. Then does this lead us to believe Morgan Prescott had the occasional wager, or that the man was an inveterate gambler? A gambler who, like so many others, found himself in hock to a rapacious turf account intent on recouping money owed to his dubious line of business?'

'Then which is it?' asked the colonel.

'Neither. At least, not in the sense of a traditional bookie, or wager,' said the inspector, mopping his brow with a hand-kerchief as he attempted to dodge the morning sun now streaming through three enormous windows. 'We believe he owed not money, but information he failed to deliver, and for which he had been paid handsomely. Morgan Prescott was in fear for his life. So, what is a man to do in such circumstances? Why not reach out to a good friend? Perhaps it wasn't the first time he'd placed such an advert. A code, one might say, to alert his friend to his plight.'

'It all sounds dubious to me, you know, personal messages written in code?'

Lemuel Norris' intervention made the inspector smile. 'Ah, Mr Norris, there you are. We shall come to you later.'

Now it became Lemuel's turn to receive the room's attention, which he did not appear to appreciate.

'Well,' continued Whipple. 'That all depends on who it is you owe the money to. We don't think Morgan Prescott owed anything to a turf accountant. Given the appearance of the fellow who warned you all off ever mentioning Morgan's name again, it's our contention that he had a private source of income. Alas, this was not family money, but a line of credit that came with strings.'

'A spy, you mean?' shouted the colonel. 'How splendid.'

Whipple shook his head. 'Not for Mr Prescott, Colonel. There may be something in what you say, though what secrets he might have been passing to whom, we shall never know.'

I noticed Augustine twitch at mention of spies and thought this most peculiar.

'We three also received a visit from a gentleman whose identity I'm not at liberty to disclose, even to my fellow investigators on this case. Let us call him Pinstripe.' HG offered a fond smile to Whipple and me. 'This gentleman arranged for two fellows to track poor Morgan. Unknown to the deceased, the man whose name I cannot speak knew about the arrangement Morgan Prescott had with Ambrose Bagley. We suspect Ambrose kept a regular eye on the personal column of that newspaper to check whether his friend remained safe or once again needed his help.'

HG proceeded to read out the cryptic message to the crowd. 'As for the reference to "W. Halt", that confused us at first, until one thinks laterally. What if "W. Halt" refers not to a name but to a meeting place: Whiston Halt train station, the nearest station to this fine manor, a confirmation of Prescott's time and place of arrival.'

The colonel shook his head. 'Forgive me, Eleanor, but you're talking in riddles.'

'Then allow me to explain further,' said the inspector, now taking over the exposition. 'There is a scribble on the back of that scrap of paper. At first, it made little sense, less still to be of importance to our investigation. But it isn't a mere scribble.'

Whipple asked for the paper from HG and retrieved a small magnifying glass from his pocket. Handing both to the guest nearest him, he bade the lady examine the markings.

'I think... yes, it is. It is a drawing of a telephone.'

Whipple smiled. 'Indeed, it is, madam. Which tells us Ambrose Bagley rang Morgan Prescott to confirm arrangements. Perhaps he didn't ring earlier for fear that Mr Prescott's telephone was being tapped. You see, Ambrose asked the butler to prepare a room and Morgan Prescott turned up. Alas, they were never to meet.'

Her Grace approached Lemuel Norris. 'You believe in destiny, do you not?'

Lemuel, still reeling from being the focus of Whipple's earlier attention, chose not to reply.

'Yet, there remained a puzzle. Although two bodies were found, their bags were not. Is it likely a gentleman would attend a weekend party without a change of clothes?' Whipple coughed and mopped his brow again.

'No, it isn't,' continued HG. 'And it's this that leads us to believe the gentleman who spoke to you about Morgan Prescott was under orders, with two others, to remove any evidence of contact between the two. In Ambrose's case, it was likely he had an enormous amount of cash in his bag that they did not want the police looking into. How they missed this small piece of paper in Ambrose's wallet or the scrap of paper we found on the floor near Morgan's body can mean only one thing. They didn't know Prescott was dead until they arrived by car on Friday morning. It saved them a job, you might say. They were playing catch-up and rushed their work. Instead of carrying out a thorough search, they removed the men's suitcases and left it at that.'

'You mean those awful fellows were on my land all the time?' said the colonel.

'Yes, they were,' replied HG. 'Which explains why the gentleman I spoke of arrived by train only yesterday. We must surmise one of the men rang their superior to explain what had happened, requiring his presence to put the matter to bed, so to speak.' I took note to observe Augustine as the dowager mentioned the station. She did not look at all comfortable, yet disguised matters by appearing disinterested in events and admiring the porcelain teacup before her.

'Our guess,' continued Whipple, 'is that his men had already arrived via his Daimler motor car to recover intelligence of some sort from Prescott, who, I suspect, had received handsome payment to secure and then pass on secret information on certain security matters to Pinstripe. Morgan Prescott must have known failure to deliver might mean death, except, of course, Ambrose Bagley complicated things by getting himself murdered. Once Pinstripe's men realised their target was also dead, what were they to do? My hunch is that they needed to make sure Morgan Prescott's room was clear of any remaining items belonging to that unfortunate man. After Mr Lomas caught them lurking outside and ordered them away, they tried a bolder approach, only to be faced with Her Grace in full swagger. What I am certain of is that they wasted no time in informing their superior of developments.'

The room fell into silence as the full implications of Whipple's oration sank in.

'Let me be clear,' said the inspector. 'What happened to Ambrose Bagley and Morgan Prescott had nothing to do with these men, although, to recap, we think Prescott was in mortal danger from them. No, the person responsible for their deaths is in this room.'

This shocking revelation stunned the gathering into an immediate silence.

At length, Watkins-Simms was the first to speak. 'Then for heaven's sake, Chief Inspector, let us get to the heart of things. Who is the murderer?'

I watched as Whipple gave an enigmatic smile. 'Ah, Mr Watkins-Simms, the older brother, the one who gives the impression of being at the sharp end of his brother's tongue... and not only his tongue.'

'What is that supposed to mean, Inspector?'

Without hesitation, Whipple launched his onslaught. 'You are both lovers of tennis, are you not? In fact, your brother did his best to inflict a severe injury on you on Saturday, did he not?'

'That's ridiculous.'

'Is it? It isn't only tennis balls that may cause injury. The racket might be a deadly weapon in capable hands, might it not? What if you were at your wit's end of being, and forgive me for mixing metaphors, a punch bag for your brother's jealousy at not inheriting his father's title for the sake of eleven minutes? What if you struck out at a completely innocent Ambrose Bagley? Yes, that's it. You had some sort of argument with the man by the lake and struck him with your racket.'

The room erupted into chaos as Watkins-Simms the younger got to his feet. 'Have you lost your senses, Chief

Inspector? My brother is incapable of such violence. Yes, we argue, but there is nothing dearer to me in this world, apart from my wife, than my twin.'

The room's attention switched from one twin to the other, then to the inspector.

'I believe you.'

'What?'

'I believe you, Mr Watkins-Simms. I simply wished to see how you might react to my hypothesis. Your delightful spouses said as much when we spoke to them. You're fortunate you both have such wonderful wives looking after your interests. I would, however, caution you on one element of your defence. We all, and I mean every human, have the capacity for evil and extreme violence. Each of us has the capacity to murder. I see the results all too often.'

HG clearly decided not to allow the pace to slow as she once again walked over to Lemuel's chair, standing a foot or so behind the fellow she asked if he had such feelings.

Although he couldn't see the dowager, the man knew who spoke. 'I've told you, I had nothing to do with the death of either of those unfortunate men.' He looked around the table, as if seeking support from his peer group. Instead, they fixed their eyes on the fellow without letting slip if any considered him innocent or guilty.

'You hated Ambrose Bagley. He stood in the way of the woman you both loved. Passion is the most intense of all feelings and can lead people to do things that, in normal circumstances, might be abhorrent to them. As the chief inspector said, we are all capable of the most heinous of crimes.'

Lemuel stood.

'Sit down,' said the inspector in a firm tone.

'You mean the poem? I told you it wasn't for the kitchen

girl. I'd seen her talking to Rowena and thought she might deliver my note, but each time I tried to approach she misunderstood my intentions.'

HG smiled, although Lemuel was not to know this as she continued to stand directly behind him. 'You make my point, Mr Norris.'

At this, Norris slumped in his chair, as if devoid of energy.

'I believe you, also,' said the chief inspector.

A gasp filled the room as Lemuel immediately regained his former stature. 'Then... why—'

'Why put you through that?' began Whipple. 'Because thinking someone is innocent isn't the same as knowing. I come across many accomplished liars in my line of business, Mr Norris. Occasionally even I'm taken in by their web of deceit. But more often I can spot a liar at ten paces. A touch of the chin, fingers covering the mouth as they speak, failure to keep eye contact when exposed to the truth. All these things tell me I'm being lied to. In your case, you exhibit no such trait, besides which we know your movements for Friday. Servants are a mine of information, you know. Little passes without them knowing. On this occasion, you should be thankful for that.'

'So that leaves us but one suspect, doesn't it, Peregrine?'

HG had a habit of making an impact. However, this time she excelled. Before the room had time to react, the colonel was on his feet again.

'Eleanor, have you lost all sense? Why do you accuse my son of such a thing?'

As his father spoke, Peregrine remained silent and unruffled. Instead, he perused a pocket-sized copy of the *Botanist's Almanac for 1922* without lifting his eyes from its pages.

'Because, Colonel, as you said yourself, your son has shown his tendency to violence from a young age, he observes visitors and your staff from a distance and oh, yes, we found a fob watch belonging to Ambrose Bagley in his room.'

Only now did Peregrine stir as pandemonium broke out all around. 'A watch? What is that you accuse me of, Your Grace? I don't own a timepiece since I follow the sun's direction. Why then should I conceal a watch in my room?'

'I didn't say you concealed it, Peregrine.'

The fellow's blood was up. 'Do not play with me, Your Grace. You may be of high station, but you're a guest in this house and not at liberty to besmirch the son of your host.'

His rattled response amounted to more words than I'd heard him speak to date. However, his new-found irritability cut no ice with the dowager.

'Two men are dead, Peregrine. That gives me the right, working under the chief inspector's authority, to make such enquiries as I see fit. Now, how did you come to possess that pocket watch, because mark my words, if you don't speak the truth now, prison may await with the dread consequence that might lead to. Do you wish to hang? Think carefully what you say next.'

Peregrine picked up his almanac as if ready to ignore the dowager's warning and begin reading from it again. He clearly thought better of the idea as he set it down on the table and relaxed back into his chair. 'Your Grace, I've no knowledge of this item. I have no need of such things. My world comprises God's bounty, not shiny objects. But you are correct. I have great difficulty in holding a conversation, looking others in the eye, even forming my words some-times. I know not why this is and yes, I did a terrible thing to

Mr Price's father, though I lost control of the horse; I did not intend to harm the man.

'However, no one believed me then, and I suspect, still to this day. I trust you'll understand that I found it easier to keep my distance. As you can see, my intentions remain misunderstood.'

His compelling oration garnered a deal of sympathy from his father's guests. I, too, began to re-evaluate this man. What if his outward presentation to the world was not one of intent to cause distress and harm but some mental incapacity to communicate verbally or form friendships? How might one live with such a burden?

In an unexpected move, the dowager stepped over to the colonel's son and placed a hand on his shoulder. The sensation of human touch appeared to send shock waves through Peregrine's body as he broke down.

'There. It's done, Peregrine. You are not our killer. However, if we have done one thing this morning, it's to allow you to truly express yourself, perhaps truly for the first time in your life.'

She gave the colonel and Augustine each a severe look, which their shaken appearance told me they well understood.

HG turned and nodded to the chief inspector. On cue, he left the room, as arranged between us.

'And so, it's time to inform you all who murdered one man and inadvertently caused the demise of a second. Isn't that true, Miss Rowena Dosett?'

Not a sound broke the awful silence as people turned to a young woman who had been quietly weeping for some thirty minutes.

'You can stop that now, Rowena.'

Miss Dosett gave her eyes a final dab with her fine cotton

kerchief before concealing it inside a cuff. 'Why do you say such a terrible thing, Your Grace? Have I not lost the love of my life, whom you now accuse me of killing? Have I not been attacked in my bed? And did you not discover evidence of Peregrine's guilt?'

The dowager smiled. 'You are a most accomplished actress, Miss Dosett. Except your undoing lies in that very talent. When you ran from the house into the chief inspector's arms saying you had suffered an attack, you had us taken in. Even when we put you to bed, watched over by a member of staff, we believed you. But that little trick with the blood on your pillow, well, you were being too clever.'

'I don't know what you mean, Your Grace. A man attacked me with something and cut my head. The blood dripped onto my pillow. You saw it?'

HR jumped at Rowena's words. 'And by that statement, you condemn yourself. Thanks to the expertise of the chief inspector, he pointed out to Rex and me that the blood pattern was not that of one dripping from the victim's wound. Instead, it proves you smeared a forefinger with blood from a self-inflicted injury onto the pillow.

'Also, the tear-drop shape of the smear proved you were out of bed. You placed your finger onto the pillow, causing an accumulation of blood, then pulled it back toward the edge of the bed. What took you a fraction of a second to complete, undid your fanciful tale of an attacker.'

Rowena stood and cried again. 'But, Your Grace, someone hit me, I swear.'

HG smiled again. 'Yes, you speak the truth, Rowena. However, that person was you. How do I know? Well, let me take you back to the bedroom we put you in. You'll remember me coming to comfort you? You asked that I help you disguise the injury with make-up.

'You were sloppy in covering your tracks, Rowena. When you handed me your compact, I noticed a tiny trace of blood in the hinge. A police constable is retrieving it from your room at this moment. No doubt when tested, it will belong to the same blood group as your good self.'

'You have no evidence,' said Rowena with a hard edge to her speech pattern.

'Au contraire, mon cheri. If you might be so good as to look toward that window?'

Everyone followed HG's invitation. Two figures stared back at them from the outside. One, the familiar figure of the chief inspector. By his side stood an unshaven gentleman pointing and nodding at Miss Dosett.

'Not only did you fake your own attack, but you covered up your dreadful crime by attempting to implicate Peregrine by hiding the watch you snatched from Ambrose Bagley's body.'

Peregrine gazed at Rowena without moving a muscle, before standing and leaving the room. HG suggested we shouldn't stop the fellow.

'You were seen, Rowena. You argued with Ambrose. Did he refuse your love? Perhaps you offered him a small gift that you snatched back after striking him, hence his outstretched hand. I'm only surprised you didn't frame a Watkins-Simms twin for your crime, since you struck Ambrose on the head with the edge of a tennis racket.'

Rowena's face flushed. 'I showed Ambrose my grandmother's engagement ring. I wanted us to use it for our own wedding, but he said he didn't want to marry. I got so angry and yes, I hit him with the racket, but not to kill him.'

The dowager turned to Dr Griffiths who'd sat quietly throughout the morning. 'Perhaps you might help us, Doctor?'

Griffiths stood to address his audience. 'From the early results of his post-mortem, I think it safe to say that Ambrose Bagley suffered from a condition we call calvarial thinning. Basically, a thinning of the skull. He would not have known this. In normal circumstances, a blow such as he suffered might cause concussion and require a few stitches at most. In his case, the blow caused instant death. Literally, he'd not have known what hit him, hence the poor fellow's strange body position when found.'

'I didn't murder him. It was an accident, that's all.'

HG rounded on Miss Dosett. 'You were not to know about his condition. You assumed you had killed the man, took back your ring from his still-warm hand and snatched the gold fob watch from his waistcoat, perhaps as a strange memento.'

Rowena shook her head, her face contorted with anger. 'But I had nothing to do with the other one.'

HG played with her pearl neckless. 'As the chief inspector said earlier, actions have consequences. You were heard arguing with another man after you left Ambrose's body, presumably to make your way back to the house as if nothing had happened.

'That man was Morgan Prescott. He came to Bircham Manor to seek sanctuary from his good friend who, he hoped, might facilitate his escape from two ruthless killers working for an insidious individual. Instead, Mr Prescott met his death. He saw you attack Ambrose and tried to take his watch back. Again, you lashed out with the tennis racket and caught him with a glancing blow as the gold chain became dislodged from the watch and fell to the ground, where we found it.

'The witness who heard the altercation came to investigate the argument he heard, only to find Morgan stumbling at the water's edge, mumbling incoherently. Assuming the man was drunk, our witness left him to it, except as I know Dr Griffiths will attest, the blow you struck caused severe concussion. The man didn't know where he was and stumbled into the lake. Unfortunately for him, at that precise location, the bank falls sharply away to deeper water. The poor fellow didn't stand a chance. The bruising to Prescott's hands confused us at first. We now know the cause of these to be his attempt to protect his head from your savage blow. However, the one thing we cannot attribute to you is the cut on the unfortunate man's right hand. It seems the colonel's rapacious pike, colloquially known as Razor-Gob, added a final insult to Morgan Prescott's miserable death.'

Just then, the chief inspector re-entered the room with two constables following.

'Rowena Bagley. I arrest you in the King's name for the murder of Ambrose Bagley and manslaughter of Morgan Prescott. Constables, get her out of my sight.'

———

PICNICKING IN THE LATE MORNING SUN, HAVING WITNESSED the aftermath of two deaths, might appear strange to some. Yet the dowager thought it a perfect antidote to the distasteful events of earlier in the day.

As Mable and I exchanged meaningful glances while laying out the picnic by the Japanese teahouse, HG and the inspector chatted away as if on a yearly vacation to Bognor Regis.

Meanwhile, the two constables busied themselves with two female house staff, having safely delivered their prisoner to the local police station to await her shackled journey to Scotland Yard.

Food and drink distributed, and all settled on a large wool blanket from the Rolls-Royce, we could, at last, enjoy each other's company without the thought of murder and mayhem.

'Come on, Eleanor, tell me about this ward of yours. What's the score?'

HG smiled as she took a sip of her lemonade. 'Why don't you tell the Inspector, Rex?'

Mable gestured encouragement with her hand and gave me the widest of smiles.

'As I told you, my father came upon hard times and had to leave me at Horizons. Of course, I didn't know what the place was, or who ran it. Nor did I realise I'd never see my father again. And so, I found myself a fourteen-year-old on my own.'

'He was such a naughty boy,' said HG. 'Always getting into fights, sticking up for some poor wretch or other, yet he excelled in our theatre productions. He always seemed to play the lead, much like his father, I expect. I also imagine that's where you came across him, Arthur... and why you recognised him when first you met.'

The man looked puzzled. 'But, Eleanor, we've been working together on and off for years. Why have I never seen him at Drakeford Old Hall? Where have you been hiding him?'

The dowager's eyes sparkled. 'I watched this young man as he grew older, taking more and more responsibilities for the younger ones. I gave him an education and, although he didn't know it, looked after him as my ward. And that's what happened. For much of the time, he remained at Horizons or was away at school. Then, for the last two years, two years in which, I should add, you have deigned not to visit me, he made his home at the hall.'

Suitably chastised for his non-attendance, Whipple blushed, while HG, Mable and I laughed to the point of having tears run down our cheeks.

'You mean I've got two of you to contend with from now on?'

'Hush, Arthur,' said the dowager. 'Here, have another iced fancy.'

ENGLISH (UK) TO US GLOSSARY

Beef Wellington: A meat dish comprising a portion of fillet steak coated in a pate and wrapped in puff pastry. Named in honour of the famous nineteen century British military man, the Duke of Wellington, although similar dishes pre-date his life.

Boiled sweet: Candy comprising mainly sugar, syrup and flavouring, boiled and shaped on cooling to make a glossy, highly coloured treat.

Car bonnet: Hood.

Cuffed me one: An old-fashioned term meaning to hit someone around the ears or across the back of the head.

Cumberland sausage: Minced pork mixed with sage, thyme, pepper and nutmeg with rusk used as a binder and served in a tight spiral shape (like a rope wound around itself when laid on the floor).

Debrett's: A long-standing annual publication representing a 'who's who' of society.

Eton Mess: An eponymous dish named after the famous English public school, comprising a mixture of strawberries, broken meringue and whipped double cream, first mentioned in 1893.

Filch: To steal. Usually an item of little or small value.

Football: Soccer.

Gob: Slang for mouth.

Gobstopper: A ball-shaped candy approximately an inch in diameter.

Guff: An old slang term to describe someone talking nonsense or an untruth. 'Don't give me that guff'.

Half-a-crown: A silver coin worth one-eighth of a British pound, which ceased circulation in 1971 when the UK changed from its 240 pennies in a pound system to a decimal system of 100 pennies, making one 'new' penny worth 2.4 'old pennies'.

Jib door: An internal door decorated to look like the rest of the room.

Nark: An old-fashioned term for a police informant.

Penny dreadful: Nineteenth century term for stories sold in weekly instalments for one penny.

Public school: Confusingly, these are 'private' schools where a termly fee is payable.

Presented at court: Until 1958, upper-class girls attended an event at Buckingham Palace in London where they were 'presented' to the king and queen to signal their 'coming out': a change in status from that of a child to an adult.

Quid: An old-fashioned term for the sum of one British pound. 'It'll cost a quid.'

Scotland Yard: The traditional London home of the Metropolitan Police.

Tap: Faucet.

Tied cottage: A house or cottage owned by a farmer or factory owner who rents it to their employee. When the employee moves on, cannot work or dies, the family must move out to allow the 'new' employee and their family to occupy it.

Turf accountant: A person or organisation who take bets at an event. Horseracing, for example.

Two-up, Two-down: A Victorian working-class house constructed in a terrace that comprised a small living room and kitchen downstairs with two bedrooms upstairs. The toilet was outside in 'the yard'. Many such buildings survive and are extended to include indoor facilities.

Whitehall: The London geographic location of the British Government. Whitehall was the traditional seat of royal power for many centuries.

DID YOU ENJOY A POSH MURDER?

Reviews are so important in helping get my books noticed. Genuine reviews of my writing help me become a better author and bring my books to the attention of new readers.

If you enjoyed my book, please spare a couple of minutes to head over to my Amazon page to leave a review (as short or long as you like).

Thank you!

With my best wishes,

Keith

JOIN MY READERS' CLUB

Getting to know my readers is the thing I like most about writing. From time to time I publish a newsletter with details of my new releases, special offers and other information I hope you will find informative and fun.

So, here's your invitation to join my readers' club – no charge, no upsells and no obligation... but if you do decide to join, I'll send you a free copy of my gripping short story, *A Record of Deceit* from my Norfolk Cozy Mystery series, with bonus content including interviews with the four lead characters.

Just head over to www.keithfinney.co.uk and sign up for my newsletter. That's all there is to it!

For Joan, who is always there for me

ACKNOWLEDGMENTS

Cover design by Books Covered

Development Editor: Alice Rees alicereesediting.com

My wonderful Advance Readers - Team Sleuth', in particular Peter R for much sterling work early on in keeping me on track. Also to Peter B, Jo, Karen, Eleanor, Pauline and Ann. I am so fortunate to have you all take such an interest in my writing, for which I thank you so much.

ALSO BY KEITH FINNEY

In the Norfolk Cozy Mystery Series

Dead Man's Trench

Murder by Hanging

The Boathouse Killer

Miller's End

Dead Again

A Yuletide Mystery

Compilation Books One to Three

Compilation Books Four to Six

In the Lipton St Faith Mysteries: Published by Lume Books

A Deadly Coincidence (On preorder sale 15 April 2021)

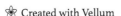 Created with Vellum

Printed in Great Britain
by Amazon